Tuck Everlasting

NATALIE BABBITT

SCHOLASTIC INC.

New York   Toronto   London   Auckland   Sydney
Mexico City   New Delhi   Hong Kong

ISBN 0-590-98886-7

36 35 34 33 32 31 30 29 28 27   2/0

Tuck Everlasting

Prologue

The first week of August hangs at the very top of summer, the top of the live-long year, like the highest seat of a Ferris wheel when it pauses in its turning. The weeks that come before are only a climb from balmy spring, and those that follow a drop to the chill of autumn, but the first week of August is motionless, and hot. It is curiously silent, too, with blank white dawns and glaring noons, and sunsets smeared with too much color. Often at night there is lightning, but it quivers all alone. There is no thunder, no relieving rain. These are strange and breathless days, the dog days, when people are led to do things they are sure to be sorry for after.

One day at that time, not so very long ago, three things happened and at first there appeared to be no connection between them.

At dawn, Mae Tuck set out on her horse for the wood at the edge of the village of Treegap. She was going there, as she did once every ten years, to meet her two sons, Miles and Jesse.

At noontime, Winnie Foster, whose family owned the Treegap wood, lost her patience at last and decided to think about running away.

And at sunset a stranger appeared at the Fosters' gate. He was looking for someone, but he didn't say who.

No connection, you would agree. But things can come together in strange ways. The wood was at the center, the hub of the wheel. All wheels must have a hub. A Ferris wheel has one, as the sun is the hub of the wheeling calendar. Fixed points they are, and best left undisturbed, for without them, nothing holds together. But sometimes people find this out too late.

1

The road that led to Treegap had been trod out long before by a herd of cows who were, to say the least, relaxed. It wandered along in curves and easy angles, swayed off and up in a pleasant tangent to the top of a small hill, ambled down again between fringes of bee-hung clover, and then cut sidewise across a meadow. Here its edges blurred. It widened and seemed to pause, suggesting tranquil bovine picnics: slow chewing and thoughtful contemplation of the infinite. And then it went on again and came at last to the wood. But on reaching the shadows of the first trees, it veered sharply, swung out in a wide arc as if, for the first time, it had reason to think where it was going, and passed around.

On the other side of the wood, the sense of easiness dissolved. The road no longer belonged to the cows. It became, instead, and rather abruptly, the property of people. And all at once the sun was uncomfortably hot, the dust oppressive, and the meager grass along its edges somewhat ragged and forlorn. On the left stood the first house, a square and solid cottage with a touch-me-not appearance, surrounded by grass cut painfully to the quick and enclosed by a capable iron fence some four feet high which clearly said, "Move on—we don't want *you* here." So the road went humbly by and made its way, past cottages more and more frequent but less and less forbidding, into the village. But the village doesn't matter, except for the jailhouse and the gallows. The first house only is important; the first house, the road, and the wood.

There was something strange about the wood. If the look of the first house suggested that you'd better pass it by, so did the look of the wood, but for quite a different reason. The house was so proud of itself that you wanted to make a lot of noise as you passed, and maybe even throw a rock or two. But the wood had a sleeping, otherworld appearance that made you want to speak in whispers. This, at least, is what the cows must have thought: "Let it keep its peace; *we* won't disturb it."

Whether the people felt that way about the wood or not is difficult to say. There were some, perhaps, who did. But for the most part the people followed the road around the wood because that was the way it led. There was no road *through* the wood. And anyway, for the people, there was another reason to leave the wood to itself: it belonged to the Fosters, the owners of the touch-me-not cottage, and was therefore private property in spite of the fact that it lay outside the fence and was perfectly accessible.

The ownership of land is an odd thing when you come to think of it. How deep, after all, can it go? If a person owns a piece of land, does he own it all the way down, in ever narrowing dimensions, till it meets all other pieces at the center of the earth? Or does ownership consist only of a thin crust under which the friendly worms have never heard of trespassing?

In any case, the wood, being on top—except, of course, for its roots—was owned bud and bough by the Fosters in the touch-me-not cottage, and if they never went there, if they never wandered in among the trees, well, that was their affair. Winnie, the only child of the house, never went there, though she sometimes stood inside the fence, carelessly banging a stick against the iron bars, and looked at it. But she had never been curious about it. Nothing ever seems interesting when it belongs to you—only when it doesn't.

And what is interesting, anyway, about a slim few acres of trees? There will be a dimness shot through with bars of sunlight, a great many squirrels and birds, a deep, damp mattress of leaves on the ground, and all the other things just as familiar if not so pleasant—things like spiders, thorns, and grubs.

In the end, however, it was the cows who were responsible for the wood's isolation, and the cows, through some wisdom they were not wise enough to know that they possessed, were very wise indeed. If they had made their road through the wood instead of around it, then the people would have followed the road. The people would have noticed the giant ash tree at the center of the wood, and then, in time, they'd have noticed the little spring bubbling up among its roots in spite of the pebbles piled there to conceal it. And that would have been a disaster so immense that this weary old earth, owned or not to its fiery core, would have trembled on its axis like a beetle on a pin.

2

And so, at dawn, that day in the first week of August, Mae Tuck woke up and lay for a while beaming at the cobwebs on the ceiling. At last she said aloud, "The boys'll be home tomorrow!"

Mae's husband, on his back beside her, did not stir. He was still asleep, and the melancholy creases that folded his daytime face were smoothed and slack. He snored gently, and for a moment the corners of his mouth turned upward in a smile. Tuck almost never smiled except in sleep.

Mae sat up in bed and looked at him tolerantly. "The boys'll be home tomorrow," she said again, a little more loudly.

Tuck twitched and the smile vanished. He opened his eyes. "Why'd you have to wake me up?" he sighed. "I was having that dream again, the good one where we're all in heaven and never heard of Treegap."

Mae sat there frowning, a great potato of a woman with a round, sensible face and calm brown eyes. "It's no use having that dream," she said. "Nothing's going to change."

"You tell me that every day," said Tuck, turning away from her onto his side. "Anyways, I can't help what I dream."

"Maybe not," said Mae. "But, all the same, you should've got used to things by now."

Tuck groaned. "I'm going back to sleep," he said.

"Not me," said Mae. "I'm going to take the horse and go down to the wood to meet them."

"Meet who?"

"The boys, Tuck! Our sons. I'm going to ride down to meet them."

"Better not do that," said Tuck.

"I know," said Mae, "but I just can't wait to see them. Anyways, it's ten years since I went to Treegap. No one'll remember me. I'll ride in at sunset, just to the wood. I won't go into the village. But, even if someone did see me, they won't remember. They never did before, now, did they?"

"Suit yourself, then," said Tuck into his pillow. "I'm going back to sleep."

Mae Tuck climbed out of bed and began to dress: three petticoats, a rusty brown skirt with one enormous pocket, an old cotton jacket, and a knitted shawl which she pinned across her bosom with a tarnished metal brooch. The sounds of her dressing were so familiar to Tuck that he could say, without opening his eyes, "You don't need that shawl in the middle of the summer."

Mae ignored this observation. Instead, she said, "Will you be all right? We won't get back till late tomorrow."

Tuck rolled over and made a rueful face at her. "What in the world could possibly happen to me?"

"That's so," said Mae. "I keep forgetting."

"*I* don't," said Tuck. "Have a nice time." And in a moment he was asleep again.

Mae sat on the edge of the bed and pulled on a pair of short leather boots so thin and soft with age it was a wonder they held together. Then she stood and took from the washstand beside the bed a little square-shaped object, a music box painted with roses and lilies of the valley. It was the one pretty thing she owned and she never went anywhere without it. Her fingers strayed to the winding key on its bottom, but glancing at the sleeping Tuck, she shook her head, gave the little box a pat, and dropped it into her pocket. Then, last of all, she pulled down over her ears a blue straw hat with a drooping, exhausted brim.

But, before she put on the hat, she brushed her

gray-brown hair and wound it into a bun at the back of her neck. She did this quickly and skillfully without a single glance in the mirror. Mae Tuck didn't need a mirror, though she had one propped up on the washstand. She knew very well what she would see in it; her reflection had long since ceased to interest her. For Mae Tuck, and her husband, and Miles and Jesse, too, had all looked exactly the same for eighty-seven years.

3

At noon of that same day in the first week of August, Winnie Foster sat on the bristly grass just inside the fence and said to the large toad who was squatting a few yards away across the road, "I will, though. You'll see. Maybe even first thing tomorrow, while everyone's still asleep."

It was hard to know whether the toad was listening or not. Certainly, Winnie had given it good reason to ignore her. She had come out to the fence, very cross, very near the boiling point on a day that was itself near to boiling, and had noticed the toad at once. It was the only living thing in sight except for a stationary cloud of hysterical gnats suspended in the heat above the road. Winnie had found some pebbles at the base of the fence and, for lack of any other way to show how she felt, had flung one at the toad. It missed altogether, as she'd fully intended it should, but she made a game of it anyway, tossing pebbles at such an angle that they passed through the gnat cloud on their way to the toad. The gnats were too frantic to notice these intrusions, however, and since every pebble missed its final mark, the toad continued to squat and grimace without so much as a twitch. Possibly it felt resentful. Or perhaps it was only asleep. In either case, it gave her not a glance when at last she ran out of pebbles and sat down to tell it her troubles.

"Look here, toad," she said, thrusting her arms through the bars of the fence and plucking at the weeds on the other side. "I don't think I can stand it much longer."

At this moment a window at the front of the cottage was flung open and a thin voice—her grandmother's—piped, "Winifred! Don't sit on that dirty grass. You'll stain your boots and stockings."

And another, firmer voice—her mother's—added, "Come in now, Winnie. Right away. You'll get heat stroke out there on a day like this. And your lunch is ready."

"See?" said Winnie to the toad. "That's just what I mean. It's like that every minute. If I had a sister or a brother, there'd be someone else for them to watch. But, as it is, there's only me. I'm tired of being looked at all the time. I want to be by myself for a change." She leaned her forehead against the bars and after a short silence went on in a thoughtful tone. "I'm not exactly sure what I'd do, you know, but something interesting—something that's all mine. Something that would make some kind of difference in the world. It'd be nice to have a new name, to start with, one that's not all worn out from being called so much. And I might even decide to have a pet. Maybe a big old toad, like you, that I could keep in a nice cage with lots of grass, and . . ."

At this the toad stirred and blinked. It gave a heave of muscles and plopped its heavy mudball of a body a few inches farther away from her.

"I suppose you're right," said Winnie. "Then you'd be just the way I am, now. Why should you have to be cooped up in a cage, too? It'd be better if I could be like you, out in the open and making up my own mind. Do you know they've hardly ever let me out of this yard all by myself? I'll never be able to do anything important if I stay in here like this. I expect I'd better run away." She paused and peered anxiously at the toad to see how it would receive this staggering idea, but it showed no signs of interest. "You think I wouldn't dare, don't you?" she said accusingly. "I will, though. You'll see. Maybe even first thing in the morning, while everyone's still asleep."

"Winnie!" came the firm voice from the window.

"All *right!* I'm coming!" she cried, exasperated, and then added quickly, "I mean, I'll be right there, Mama." She stood up, brushing at her legs where bits of itchy grass clung to her stockings.

The toad, as if it saw that their interview was over, stirred again, bunched up, and bounced itself clumsily off toward the wood. Winnie watched it go. "Hop away, toad," she called after it. "You'll see. Just wait till morning."

4

At sunset of that same long day, a stranger came strolling up the road from the village and paused at the Fosters' gate. Winnie was once again in the yard, this time intent on catching fireflies, and at first she didn't notice him. But, after a few moments of watching her, he called out, "Good evening!"

He was remarkably tall and narrow, this stranger standing there. His long chin faded off into a thin, apologetic beard, but his suit was a jaunty yellow that seemed to glow a little in the fading light. A black hat dangled from one hand, and as Winnie came toward him, he passed the other through his dry, gray hair, settling it smoothly. "Well, now," he said in a light voice. "Out for fireflies, are you?"

"Yes," said Winnie.

"A lovely thing to do on a summer evening," said the man richly. "A lovely entertainment. I used to do it myself when I was your age. But of course that was a long, long time ago." He laughed, gesturing in self-deprecation with long, thin fingers. His tall body moved continuously; a foot tapped, a shoulder twitched. And it moved in angles, rather jerkily. But at the same time he had a kind of grace, like a well-handled marionette. Indeed, he seemed almost to hang suspended there in the twilight. But Winnie, though she was half charmed, was suddenly reminded of the stiff black ribbons they had hung on the door of the cottage for her grandfather's funeral. She frowned and looked at the man more closely. But his smile seemed perfectly all right, quite agreeable and friendly.

"Is this your house?" asked the man, folding his arms now and leaning against the gate.

"Yes," said Winnie. "Do you want to see my father?"

"Perhaps. In a bit," said the man. "But I'd like to talk to you first. Have you and your family lived here long?"

"Oh, yes," said Winnie. "We've lived here forever."

"Forever," the man echoed thoughtfully.

It was not a question, but Winnie decided to explain anyway. "Well, not forever, of course, but as long as there've been any people here. My grandmother was born here. She says this was all trees once, just one big forest everywhere around, but it's mostly all cut down now. Except for the wood."

"I see," said the man, pulling at his beard. "So of course you know everyone, and everything that goes on."

"Well, not especially," said Winnie. "At least, *I* don't. Why?"

The man lifted his eyebrows. "Oh," he said, "I'm looking for someone. A family."

"I don't know anybody much," said Winnie, with a shrug. "But my father might. You could ask him."

"I believe I shall," said the man. "I do believe I shall."

At this moment the cottage door opened, and in the lamp glow that spilled across the grass, Winnie's grandmother appeared. "Winifred? Who are you talking to out there?"

"It's a man, Granny," she called back. "He says he's looking for someone."

"What's that?" said the old woman. She picked up her skirts and came down the path to the gate. "What did you say he wants?"

The man on the other side of the fence bowed slightly. "Good evening, madam," he said. "How delightful to see you looking so fit."

"And why shouldn't I be fit?" she retorted, peering at him through the fading light. His yellow suit seemed to surprise her, and she squinted suspiciously.

"We haven't met, that I can recall. Who are you? Who are you looking for?"

The man answered neither of these questions. Instead, he said, "This young lady tells me you've lived here for a long time, so I thought you would probably know everyone who comes and goes."

The old woman shook her head. "I *don't* know everyone," she said, "nor do I want to. And I don't stand outside in the dark discussing such a thing with strangers. Neither does Winifred. So . . ."

And then she paused. For, through the twilight sounds of crickets and sighing trees, a faint, surprising wisp of music came floating to them, and all three turned toward it, toward the wood. It was a tinkling little melody, and in a few moments it stopped.

"My stars!" said Winnie's grandmother, her eyes round. "I do believe it's come again, after all these years!" She pressed her wrinkled hands together, forgetting the man in the yellow suit. "Did you hear that, Winifred? That's it! That's the elf music I told you about. Why, it's been ages since I heard it last. And this is the first time you've *ever* heard it, isn't it? Wait till we tell your father!" And she seized Winnie's hand and turned to go back into the cottage.

"Wait!" said the man at the gate. He had stiffened, and his voice was eager. "You've heard that music before, you say?"

But, before he could get an answer, it began again and they all stopped to listen. This time it tinkled its way faintly through the little melody three times before it faded.

"It sounds like a music box," said Winnie when it was over.

"Nonsense. It's elves!" crowed her grandmother excitedly. And then she said to the man at the gate, "You'll have to excuse us now." She shook the gate latch under his nose, to make sure it was locked, and then, taking Winnie by the hand once more, she marched up the path into the cottage, shutting the door firmly behind her.

But the man in the yellow suit stood tapping his foot in the road for a long time all alone, looking at the wood. The last stains of sunset had melted away, and the twilight died, too, as he stood there, though its remnants clung reluctantly to everything that was pale in color—pebbles, the dusty road, the figure of the man himself—turning them blue and blurry.

Then the moon rose. The man came to himself and sighed. His expression was one of intense satisfaction. He put on his hat, and in the moonlight his long fingers were graceful and very white. Then he turned and disappeared down the shadowy road, and as he went he whistled, very softly, the tinkling little melody from the wood.

5

Winnie woke early next morning. The sun was only just opening its own eye on the eastern horizon and the cottage was full of silence. But she realized that sometime during the night she had made up her mind: she would not run away today. "Where would I go, anyway?" she asked herself. "There's nowhere else I really want to be." But in another part of her head, the dark part where her oldest fears were housed, she knew there was another sort of reason for staying at home: she was afraid to go away alone.

It was one thing to talk about being by yourself, doing important things, but quite another when the opportunity arose. The characters in the stories she read always seemed to go off without a thought or care, but in real life—well, the world was a dangerous place. People were always telling her so. And she would not be able to manage without protection. They were always telling her that, too. No one ever said precisely what it was that she would not be able to manage. But she did not need to ask. Her own imagination supplied the horrors.

Still, it was galling, this having to admit she was afraid. And when she remembered the toad, she felt even more disheartened. What if the toad should be out by the fence again today? What if he should laugh at her secretly and think she was a coward?

Well, anyway, she could at least slip out, right now, she decided, and go into the wood. To see if she could discover what had really made the music the night before. That would be something, anyway. She did not allow herself to consider the idea that making a difference in the world might require a bolder venture. She merely told herself consolingly, "Of course, while I'm in the wood, if I decide never to come back, well then, that will be that." She was able to believe in this because she needed to; and, believing, was her own true, promising friend once more.

It was another heavy morning, already hot and breathless, but in the wood the air was cooler and smelled agreeably damp. Winnie had been no more than two slow minutes walking timidly under the in terlacing branches when she wondered why she had never come here before. "Why, it's nice!" she thought with great surprise.

For the wood was full of light, entirely different from the light she was used to. It was green and amber and alive, quivering in splotches on the padded ground, fanning into sturdy stripes between the tree trunks. There were little flowers she did not recognize, white and palest blue; and endless, tangled vines; and here and there a fallen log, half rotted but soft with patches of sweet green-velvet moss.

And there were creatures everywhere. The air fairly hummed with their daybreak activity: beetles and birds and squirrels and ants, and countless other things unseen, all gentle and self-absorbed and not in the least alarming. There was even, she saw with satisfaction, the toad. It was squatting on a low stump and she might not have noticed it, for it looked more like a mushroom than a living creature sitting there. As she came abreast of it, however, it blinked, and the movement gave it away.

"See?" she exclaimed. "I told you I'd be here first thing in the morning."

The toad blinked again and nodded. Or perhaps it was only swallowing a fly. But then it nudged itself off the edge of the stump and vanished in the underbrush.

"It must have been watching for me," said Winnie to herself, and was very glad she had come.

She wandered for a long time, looking at everything, listening to everything, proud to forget the tight, pruned world outside, humming a little now, trying to remember the pattern of the melody she had heard the night before. And then, up ahead, in a place where the light seemed brighter and the ground somewhat more open, something moved.

Winnie stopped abruptly and crouched down. "If it's really elves," she thought, "I can have a look at them." And, though her instinct was to turn and run, she was pleased to discover that her curiosity was stronger. She began to creep forward. She would go just close enough, she told herself. Just close enough to see. And *then* she would turn and run. But when she came near, up behind a sheltering tree trunk, and peered around it, her mouth dropped open and all thought of running melted away.

There was a clearing directly in front of her, at the center of which an enormous tree thrust up, its thick roots rumpling the ground ten feet around in every direction. Sitting relaxed with his back against the trunk was a boy, almost a man. And he seemed so glorious to Winnie that she lost her heart at once.

He was thin and sunburned, this wonderful boy, with a thick mop of curly brown hair, and he wore his battered trousers and loose, grubby shirt with as much self-assurance as if they were silk and satin. A pair of green suspenders, more decorative than useful, gave the finishing touch, for he was shoeless and there was a twig tucked between the toes of one foot. He waved the twig idly as he sat there, his face turned up to gaze at the branches far above him. The golden morning light seemed to glow all around him, while brighter patches fell, now on his lean, brown hands, now on his hair and face, as the leaves stirred over his head.

Then he rubbed an ear carelessly, yawned, and stretched. Shifting his position, he turned his attention to a little pile of pebbles next to him. As Winnie watched, scarcely breathing, he moved the pile carefully to one side, pebble by pebble. Beneath the pile, the ground was shiny wet. The boy lifted a final stone and Winnie saw a low spurt of water, arching up and returning, like a fountain, into the ground. He bent and put his lips to the spurt, drinking noiselessly, and then he sat up again and drew his shirt sleeve across his mouth. As he did this, he turned his face in her direction—and their eyes met.

For a long moment they looked at each other in silence, the boy with his arm still raised to his mouth. Neither of them moved. At last his arm fell to his side. "You may as well come out," he said, with a frown.

Winnie stood up, embarrassed and, because of that, resentful. "I didn't mean to watch you," she protested as she stepped into the clearing. "I didn't know anyone would be here."

The boy eyed her as she came forward. "What're *you* doing here?" he asked her sternly.

"It's my wood," said Winnie, surprised by the question. "I can come here whenever I want to. At least, I was never here before, but I *could* have come, any time."

"Oh," said the boy, relaxing a little. "You're one of the Fosters, then."

"I'm Winnie," she said. "Who are you?"

"I'm Jesse Tuck," he answered. "How do." And he put out a hand.

Winnie took his hand, staring at him. He was even more beautiful up close. "Do you live nearby?" she managed at last, letting go of his hand reluctantly. "I never saw you before. Do you come here a lot? No one's supposed to. It's our wood." Then she added quickly, "It's all right, though, if *you* come here. I mean, it's all right with *me*."

The boy grinned. "No, I don't live nearby, and no, I don't come here often. Just passing through. And thanks, I'm glad it's all right with you."

"That's good," said Winnie irrelevantly. She stepped back and sat down primly a short distance from him. "How old are you, anyway?" she asked, squinting at him.

There was a pause. At last he said, "Why do you want to know?"

"I just wondered," said Winnie.

"All right. I'm one hundred and four years old," he told her solemnly.

"No, I mean really," she persisted.

"Well then," he said, "if you must know, I'm seventeen."

"Seventeen?"

"That's right."

"Oh," said Winnie hopelessly. "Seventeen. That's old."

"You have no idea," he agreed with a nod.

Winnie had the feeling he was laughing at her, but decided it was a nice kind of laughing. "Are you married?" she asked next.

This time he laughed out loud. "No, I'm not married. Are you?"

Now it was Winnie's turn to laugh. "Of course not," she said. "I'm only ten. But I'll be eleven pretty soon."

"And *then* you'll get married," he suggested.

Winnie laughed again, her head on one side, admiring him. And then she pointed to the spurt of water. "Is that good to drink?" she asked. "I'm thirsty."

Jesse Tuck's face was instantly serious. "Oh, that. No—no, it's not," he said quickly. "You mustn't drink from it. Comes right up out of the ground. Probably pretty dirty." And he began to pile the pebbles over it again.

"But *you* drank some," Winnie reminded him.

"Oh. Did you see that?" He looked at her anxiously. "Well, me, I'll drink anything. I mean, I'm used to it. It wouldn't be good for *you*, though."

"Why not?" said Winnie. She stood up. "It's mine, anyway, if it's in the wood. I want some. I'm about dry as dust." And she went to where he sat, and knelt down beside the pile of pebbles.

"Believe me, Winnie Foster," said Jesse, "it would be terrible for you if you drank any of this water. Just terrible. I can't let you."

"Well, I still don't see why not," said Winnie plaintively. "I'm getting thirstier every minute. If it didn't hurt you, it won't hurt me. If my papa was here, he'd let me have some."

"You're not going to tell him about it, are you?" said Jesse. His face had gone very pale under its sunburn. He stood up and put a bare foot firmly on the pile of pebbles. "I knew this would happen sooner or later. *Now* what am I going to do?"

As he said this, there was a crashing sound among the trees and a voice called, "Jesse?"

"Thank goodness!" said Jesse, blowing out his cheeks in relief. "Here comes Ma and Miles. They'll know what to do."

And sure enough, a big, comfortable-looking woman appeared, leading a fat old horse, and at her side was a young man almost as beautiful as Jesse. It was Mae Tuck with her other son, Jesse's older brother. And at once, when she saw the two of them, Jesse with his foot on the pile of pebbles and Winnie on her knees beside him, she seemed to understand. Her hand flew to her bosom, grasping at the old brooch that fastened her shawl, and her face went bleak. "Well, boys," she said, "here it is. The worst is happening at last."

6

Afterward, when she thought about it, it seemed to Winnie that the next few minutes were only a blur. First she was kneeling on the ground, insisting on a drink from the spring, and the next thing she knew, she was seized and swung through the air, open-mouthed, and found herself straddling the bouncing back of the fat old horse, with Miles and Jesse trotting along on either side, while Mae ran puffing ahead, dragging on the bridle.

Winnie had often been haunted by visions of what it would be like to be kidnapped. But none of her visions had been like this, with her kidnappers just as alarmed as she was herself. She had always pictured a troupe of burly men with long black moustaches who would tumble her into a blanket and bear her off like a sack of potatoes while she pleaded for mercy. But, instead, it was *they*, Mae Tuck and Miles and Jesse, who were pleading.

"Please, child . . . dear, dear child . . . don't you be scared." This was Mae, trying to run and call back over her shoulder at the same time. "We . . . wouldn't harm you . . . for the world."

"If you'd . . . yelled or anything"—this was Jesse —"someone might've heard you and . . . that's too risky."

And Miles said, "We'll explain it . . . soon as we're far enough away."

Winnie herself was speechless. She clung to the saddle and gave herself up to the astonishing fact that, though her heart was pounding and her backbone felt like a pipe full of cold running water, her head was fiercely calm. Disconnected thoughts presented themselves one by one, as if they had been waiting their turn in line. "So this is what it's like to ride a horse—I was going to run away today anyway—what will they say when I'm not there for breakfast—I wish the toad could see me now—that woman is worried about me—Miles is taller than Jesse—I'd better duck if I don't want this next branch to knock me off."

They had come to the edge of the wood now, with no sign of slowing their rapid jog. The road, where it angled across the meadow, was just ahead, dazzling white in the open sunlight. And there, standing on the road, was the man from the night before, the man in the yellow suit, his black hat on his head.

Discovering him, seeing his surprise, and presented at once with choices, Winnie's mind perversely went blank. Instead of crying out for help, she merely goggled at him as they fled past the spot where he stood. Mae Tuck was the only one who spoke, and the most she could offer was: "Teaching our little girl . . . how to ride!" Only then did it come to Winnie that she ought to shout, wave her arms, do *something*. But the man had fallen away behind by that time, and she was afraid to let go of the saddle, afraid to turn around, lest she fall off the horse. In another moment it was too late. They had sped up the hill and down its other side, and the opportunity was lost.

After another few minutes, the road led them to a place where, off to the left, a shallow stream looped near, with willows and sheltering, scrubby bushes. "Stop!" cried Mae. "We'll stop here!" Miles and Jesse grabbed at the horse's harness and he pulled up abruptly, nearly toppling Winnie off over his neck. "Lift the poor child down," Mae gasped, her chest heaving. "We'll go catch our breath by the water and try to put things straight before we go on."

But the explanation, once they had stumbled to the banks of the stream, came hard. Mae seemed embarrassed, and Miles and Jesse fidgeted, glancing at their mother uneasily. No one knew how to begin. For her part, Winnie, now that the running was over, began to comprehend what was happening, and with the comprehension her throat closed and her mouth went dry as paper. This was no vision. This was real. Strangers were taking her away; they might do anything; she might never see her mother again. And then, thinking of her mother, she saw herself as small, weak, and helpless, and she began to cry, suddenly, crushed as much by outrage as by shock.

Mae Tuck's round face wrinkled in dismay. "Dear Lord, don't cry! Please don't cry, child!" she implored. "We're not bad people, truly we're not. We *had* to bring you away—you'll see why in a minute —and we'll take you back just as soon as we can. Tomorrow. I promise."

When Mae said, "Tomorrow," Winnie's sobs turned to wails. Tomorrow! It was like being told she would be kept away forever. She wanted to go home now, at once, rush back to the safety of the fence and her mother's voice from the window. Mae reached out to her, but she twisted away, her hands over her face, and gave herself up to weeping.

"This is awful!" said Jesse. "Can't you do something, Ma? The poor little tad."

"We ought to've had some better plan than *this*," said Miles.

"That's the truth," said Mae helplessly. "The dear Lord knows there's been time enough to think of one, and it had to happen sooner or later. We been plain bone lucky it hasn't before now. But I never expected it'd be a *child!*" She reached distractedly into the pocket of her skirt and took out the music box and, without thinking, twisted the winding key with trembling fingers.

When the tinkling little melody began, Winnie's sobbing slowed. She stood by the stream, her hands still over her face, and listened. Yes, it was the same music she had heard the night before. Somehow it calmed her. It was like a ribbon tying her to familiar things. She thought, "When I get home, I'll tell Granny it wasn't elf music after all." She wiped her face as well as she could with her wet hands and turned to Mae. "That's the music I heard last night," she managed between recovering snuffles. "When I was out in my yard. My granny said it was elves."

"Dear me, no," said Mae, peering at her hopefully. "It's only my music box. I didn't suppose anyone could hear it." She held it out to Winnie. "Do you want to take a look at it?"

"It's pretty," said Winnie, taking the little box and turning it over in her hands. The winding key was still revolving, but more and more slowly. The melody faltered. Another few widely spaced notes plinked, and then it stopped.

"Wind it up if you want to," said Mae. "Clock-wise."

Winnie turned the key. It clicked faintly. And then, after several more turns, the music began to play again, brisk from its fresh winding, and merry. No one who owned a thing like this could be too disagreeable. Winnie examined the painted roses and lilies of the valley, and smiled in spite of herself. "It's pretty," she repeated, handing it back to Mae.

The music box had relaxed them all. Miles dragged a handkerchief from a back pocket and mopped at his face, and Mae sank down heavily on a rock, pulling off the blue straw hat and fanning herself with it.

"Look here, Winnie Foster," said Jesse. "We're friends, we really are. But you got to help us. Come sit down, and we'll try to tell you why."

7

It was the strangest story Winnie had ever heard. She soon suspected they had never told it before, except to each other—that she was their first real audience; for they gathered around her like children at their mother's knee, each trying to claim her attention, and sometimes they all talked at once, and interrupted each other, in their eagerness.

Eighty-seven years before, the Tucks had come from a long way to the east, looking for a place to settle. In those days the wood was not a wood, it was a forest, just as her grandmother had said: a forest that went on and on and on. They had thought they would start a farm, as soon as they came to the end of the trees. But the trees never seemed to end. When they came to the part that was now the wood, and turned from the trail to find a camping place, they happened on the spring. "It was real nice," said Jesse with a sigh. "It looked just the way it does now. A clearing, lots of sunshine, that big tree with all those knobby roots. We stopped and everyone took a drink, even the horse."

"No," said Mae, "the cat didn't drink. That's important."

"Yes," said Miles, "don't leave that out. We all had a drink, except for the cat."

"Well, anyway," Jesse went on, "the water tasted —sort of strange. But we camped there overnight. And Pa carved a T on the tree trunk, to mark where we'd been. And then we went on."

They had come out of the forest at last, many miles to the west, had found a thinly populated valley, had started their farm. "We put up a house for Ma and Pa," said Miles, "and a little shack for Jesse and me. We figured *we'd* be starting families of our own pretty soon and would want our own houses."

"That was the first time we figured there was something peculiar," said Mae. "Jesse fell out of a tree . . ."

"I was way up in the middle," Jesse interrupted, "trying to saw off some of the big branches before we cut her down. I lost my balance and I fell . . ."

"He landed plum on his head," said Mae with a shudder. "We thought for sure he'd broke his neck. But come to find out, it didn't hurt him a bit!"

"Not long after," Miles went on, "some hunters

come by one day at sunset. The horse was out grazing by some trees and they shot him. Mistook him for a deer, they said. Can you fancy that? But the thing is, they didn't kill him. The bullet went right on through him, and didn't hardly even leave a mark."

"Then Pa got snake bite . . ."

"And Jesse ate the poison toadstools . . ."

"And I cut myself," said Mae. "Remember? Slicing bread."

But it was the passage of time that worried them most. They had worked the farm, settled down, made friends. But after ten years, then twenty, they had to face the fact that there was something terribly wrong. None of them was getting any older.

"I was more'n forty by then," said Miles sadly. "I was married. I had two children. But, from the look of me, I was still twenty-two. My wife, she finally made up her mind I'd sold my soul to the Devil. She left me. She went away and she took the children with her."

"I'm glad *I* never got married," Jesse put in.

"It was the same with our friends," said Mae. "They come to pull back from us. There was talk about witchcraft. Black magic. Well, you can't hardly blame them, but finally we had to leave the farm. We didn't know where to go. We started back the way we come, just wandering. We was like gypsies. When we got this far, it'd changed, of course. A lot of the trees was gone. There was people, and Treegap —it was a new village. The road was here, but in those days it was mostly just a cow path. We went on into what was left of the wood to make a camp, and when we got to the clearing and the tree and the spring, we remembered it from before."

"*It* hadn't changed, no more'n we had," said Miles. "And that was how we found out. Pa'd carved a T on the tree, remember, twenty years before, but the T was just where it'd been when he done it. That tree hadn't grown one whit in all that time. It was exactly the same. And the T he'd carved was as fresh as if it'd just been put there."

Then they had remembered drinking the water. They—and the horse. But not the cat. The cat had lived a long and happy life on the farm, but had died some ten years before. So they decided at last that the source of their changelessness was the spring.

"When we come to that conclusion," Mae went on, "Tuck said—that's my husband, Angus Tuck— he said he had to be sure, once and for all. He took his shotgun and he pointed it at hisself the best way he could, and before we could stop him, he pulled the trigger." There was a long pause. Mae's fingers, laced together in her lap, twisted with the tension of remembering. At last she said, "The shot knocked him down. Went into his heart. It *had* to, the way he aimed. And right on through him. It scarcely even left a mark. Just like—*you* know—like you shot a bullet through water. And he was just the same as if he'd never done it."

"After that we went sort of crazy," said Jesse, grinning at the memory. "Heck, we was going to live forever. Can you picture what it felt like to find that out?"

"But then we sat down and talked it over . . ." said Miles.

"We're still talking it over," Jesse added.

"And we figured it'd be very bad if everyone knowed about that spring," said Mae. "We begun to see what it would mean." She peered at Winnie. "Do you understand, child? That water—it stops you right where you are. If you'd had a drink of it today, you'd stay a little girl forever. You'd never grow up, not ever."

"We don't know how it works, or even why," said Miles.

"Pa thinks it's something left over from—well, from some other plan for the way the world should be," said Jesse. "Some plan that didn't work out too good. And so everything was changed. Except that the spring was passed over, somehow or other. Maybe he's right. *I* don't know. But you see, Winnie Foster, when I told you before I'm a hundred and four years old, I was telling the truth. But I'm really only seventeen. And, so far as I know, I'll stay seventeen till the end of the world."

8

Winnie did not believe in fairy tales. She had never longed for a magic wand, did not expect to marry a prince, and was scornful—most of the time—of her grandmother's elves. So now she sat, mouth open, wide-eyed, not knowing what to make of this extraordinary story. It couldn't—not a bit of it—be true. And yet:

"It feels so fine to tell somebody!" Jesse exploded. "Just think, Winnie Foster, you're the only person in the world, besides us, who knows about it!"

"Hold on now," said Miles cautiously. "Maybe not. There might be a whole lot of others, for all we know, wandering around just like us."

"Maybe. But *we* don't know them," Jesse pointed out. "We've never had anyone but us to talk about it to. Winnie—isn't it peculiar? And kind of wonderful? Just think of all the things we've seen in the world! All the things we're going to see!"

"That kind of talk'll make her want to rush back and drink a gallon of the stuff," warned Miles. "There's a whole lot more to it than Jesse Tuck's good times, you know."

"Oh, stuff," said Jesse with a shrug. "We might as well enjoy it, long as we can't change it. You don't have to be such a parson all the time."

"I'm not being a parson," said Miles. "I just think you ought to take it more serious."

"Now, boys," said Mae. She was kneeling by the stream, splashing her face and hands with cool water. "Whew! Such weather!" she exclaimed, sitting back on her heels. She unfastened the brooch, took off her shawl, and toweled her dripping face. "Well, child," she said to Winnie, standing up, "now you share our secret. It's a big, dangerous secret. We got to have your help to keep it. I expect you're full of questions, but we can't stay here no longer." She tied the shawl around her waist then, and sighed. "It pains me to think how your ma and pa will worry, but there's just no way around it. We got to take you home with us. That's the plan. Tuck—he'll want to talk it out, make sure you see why you can't tell no one. But we'll bring you back tomorrow. All right?" And all three of them looked at her hopefully.

"All right," said Winnie. For, she decided, there

wasn't any choice. She would have to go. They would probably make her go, anyway, no matter what she said. But she felt there was nothing to be afraid of, not really. For they seemed gentle. Gentle and—in a strange way—childlike. They made her feel old. And the way they spoke to her, the way they looked at her, made her feel special. Important. It was a warm, spreading feeling, entirely new. She liked it, and in spite of their story, she liked them, too—especially Jesse.

But it was Miles who took her hand and said, "It's really fine to have you along, even if it's only for a day or two."

Then Jesse gave a great whoop and leapt into the stream, splashing mightily. "What'd you bring for breakfast, Ma?" he cried. "We can eat on the way, can't we? I'm starving!"

So, with the sun riding high now in the sky, they started off again, noisy in the August stillness, eating bread and cheese. Jesse sang funny old songs in a loud voice and swung like a monkey from the branches of trees, showing off shamelessly for Winnie, calling to her, "Hey, Winnie Foster, watch me!" and "Look what I can do!"

And Winnie, laughing at him, lost the last of her alarm. They were friends, *her* friends. She was running away after all, but she was not alone. Closing the gate on her oldest fears as she had closed the gate of her own fenced yard, she discovered the wings she'd always wished she had. And all at once she was elated. Where were the terrors she'd been told she should expect? She could not recognize them any-where. The sweet earth opened out its wide four corners to her like the petals of a flower ready to be picked, and it shimmered with light and possibility till she was dizzy with it. Her mother's voice, the feel of home, receded for the moment, and her thoughts turned forward. Why, she, too, might live forever in this remarkable world she was only just discovering! The story of the spring—it might be true! So that, when she was not rolling along on the back of the fat old horse—by choice, this time—she ran shouting down the road, her arms flung out, making more noise than anybody.

It was good. So good, in fact, that through it all, not one of them noticed that the man they had passed on the road, the man in the yellow suit, had crept up to the bushes by the stream and heard it all, the whole fantastic story. Nor did they notice that he was following now, beside the road far behind, his mouth, above the thin, gray beard, turned ever so slightly toward a smile.

9

The August sun rolled up, hung at mid-heaven for a blinding hour, and at last wheeled westward before the journey was done. But Winnie was exhausted long before that. Miles carried her some of the way. The tops of her cheeks were bright pink with sunburn, her nose a vivid, comic red, but she had been rescued from a more serious broiling by Mae, who had finally insisted that she wear the blue straw hat. It came down far over her ears and gave her a clownish appearance, but the shade from its brim was so welcome that Winnie put vanity aside and dozed gratefully in Miles's strong arms, her own arms wound around his neck.

The pastures, fields, and scrubby groves they crossed were vigorous with bees, and crickets leapt before them as if each step released a spring and flung them up like pebbles. But everything else was motionless, dry as biscuit, on the brink of burning, hoarding final reservoirs of sap, trying to hold out till the rain returned, and Queen Anne's lace lay dusty on the surface of the meadows like foam on a painted sea.

It was amazing, then, to climb a long hill, to see ahead another hill, and beyond that the deep green of a scattered pine forest, and as you climbed, to feel the air ease and soften. Winnie revived, sniffing, and was able to ride the horse again, perched behind Mae. And to her oft-repeated question, "Are we almost there?" the welcome answer came at last: "Only a few more minutes now."

A wide stand of dark pines rose up, loomed nearer, and suddenly Jesse was crying, "We're home! This is it, Winnie Foster!" And he and Miles raced on and disappeared among the trees. The horse followed, turning onto a rutted path lumpy with roots, and it was as if they had slipped in under a giant colander. The late sun's brilliance could penetrate only in scattered glimmers, and everything was silent and untouched, the ground muffled with moss and sliding needles, the graceful arms of the pines stretched out protectively in every direction. And it was cool, blessedly cool and green. The horse picked his way carefully, and then ahead the path dropped down a steep embankment; and beyond that, Winnie, peering around Mae's bulk, saw a flash of color and a dazzling sparkle. Down the embankment they swayed and there it was, a plain, homely little house, barn-red, and below it the last of the sun flashing on the wrinkled surface of a tiny lake.

"Oh, *look!*" cried Winnie. "Water!"

At the same time, they heard two enormous splashes, two voices roaring with pleasure.

"It don't take 'em more'n a minute to pile into that pond," said Mae, beaming. "Well, you can't blame 'em in heat like this. You can go in, too, if you want."

Then they were at the door of the little house and Tuck was standing there. "Where's the child?" he demanded, for Winnie was hidden behind his wife. "The boys say you brung along a real, honest-to-goodness, natural child!"

"So I did," said Mae, sliding down off the horse, "and here she is."

Winnie's shyness returned at once when she saw the big man with his sad face and baggy trousers, but as he gazed at her, the warm, pleasing feeling spread through her again. For Tuck's head tilted to one side, his eyes went soft, and the gentlest smile in the world displaced the melancholy creases of his cheeks. He reached up to lift her from the horse's back and he said, "There's just no words to tell you how happy I am to see you. It's the finest thing that's happened in . . ." He interrupted himself, setting Winnie on the ground, and turned to Mae. "Does she know?"

"Course she knows," said Mae. "That's why I brung her back. Winnie, here's my husband, Angus Tuck. Tuck, meet Winnie Foster."

"How do, Winnie Foster," said Tuck, shaking Winnie's hand rather solemnly. "Well, then!" He straightened and peered down at her, and Winnie, looking back into his face, saw an expression there that made her feel like an unexpected present, wrapped in pretty paper and tied with ribbons, in spite of Mae's blue hat, which still enveloped her head. "Well, then," Tuck repeated, "seeing you know, I'll go on and say this is the finest thing that's happened in—oh—at least eighty years."

10

Winnie had grown up with order. She was used to it. Under the pitiless double assaults of her mother and grandmother, the cottage where she lived was always squeaking clean, mopped and swept and scoured into limp submission. There was no room for carelessness, no putting things off until later. The Foster women had made a fortress out of duty. Within it, they were indomitable. And Winnie was in training.

So she was unprepared for the homely little house beside the pond, unprepared for the gentle eddies of dust, the silver cobwebs, the mouse who lived—and welcome to him!—in a table drawer. There were only three rooms. The kitchen came first, with an open cabinet where dishes were stacked in perilous towers without the least regard for their varying dimensions. There was an enormous black stove, and a metal sink, and every surface, every wall, was piled and strewn and hung with everything imaginable, from onions to lanterns to wooden spoons to washtubs. And in a corner stood Tuck's forgotten shotgun.

The parlor came next, where the furniture, loose and sloping with age, was set about helter-skelter. An ancient green-plush sofa lolled alone in the center, like yet another mossy fallen log, facing a soot-streaked fireplace still deep in last winter's ashes. The table with the drawer that housed the mouse was pushed off, also alone, into a far corner, and three armchairs and an elderly rocker stood about aimlessly, like strangers at a party, ignoring each other.

Beyond this was the bedroom, where a vast and tipsy brass bed took up most of the space, but there was room beside it for the washstand with the lonely mirror, and opposite its foot a cavernous oak wardrobe from which leaked the faint smell of camphor.

Up a steep flight of narrow stairs was a dusty loft —"That's where the boys sleep when they're home," Mae explained—and that was all. And yet it was not quite all. For there was everywhere evidence of their activities, Mae's and Tuck's. Her sewing: patches and scraps of bright cloth; half-completed quilts and braided rugs; a bag of cotton batting with wisps of its contents, like snow, drifting into cracks and corners; the arms of the sofa webbed with strands of thread and dangerous with needles. His wood carving: curly shavings furring the floor, and little heaps of splinters and chips; every surface dim with the sawdust of countless sandings; limbs of unassembled dolls and wooden soldiers; a ship model propped on the mouse's table, waiting for its glue to dry; and a stack of wooden bowls, their sides smoothed to velvet, the topmost bowl filled with a jumble of big wooden spoons and forks, like dry, bleached bones. "We make things to sell," said Mae, surveying the mess approvingly.

And still this was not all. For, on the old beamed ceiling of the parlor, streaks of light swam and danced and wavered like a bright mirage, reflected through the windows from the sunlit surface of the pond. There were bowls of daisies everywhere, gay white and yellow. And over everything was the clean, sweet smell of the water and its weeds, the chatter of a swooping kingfisher, the carol and trill of a dozen other kinds of bird, and occasionally the thrilling bass note of an unastonished bullfrog at ease somewhere along the muddy banks.

Into it all came Winnie, eyes wide, and very much amazed. It was a whole new idea to her that people could live in such disarray, but at the same time she was charmed. It was . . . comfortable. Climbing behind Mae up the stairs to see the loft, she thought to herself: "Maybe it's because they think they have forever to clean it up." And this was followed by another thought, far more revolutionary: "Maybe they just don't care!"

"The boys don't be home very much," said Mae as they came up into the half light of the loft. "But when they are, they bed up here. There's plenty of room." The loft was cluttered, too, with all kinds of odds and ends, but there were two mattresses rolled out on the floor, and fresh sheets and blankets were folded almost neatly on each, waiting to be spread.

"Where do they go when they're away?" asked Winnie. "What do they do?"

"Oh," said Mae, "they go different places, do different things. They work at what jobs they can get, try to bring home some of their money. Miles can do carpentering, and he's a pretty fair blacksmith, too. Jesse now, *he* don't ever seem too settled in himself. Course, he's young." She stopped and smiled. "That sounds funny, don't it? Still, it's true, just the same. So Jesse, he does what strikes him at the moment, working in the fields, or in saloons, things like that, whatever he comes across. But they can't stay on in any one place for long, you know. None of us can. People get to wondering." She sighed. "We been in this house about as long as we dare, going on twenty years. It's a right nice place. Tuck's got so's he's real attached to it. Then, too, it's off by itself, plenty of fish in the pond, not too far from the towns around. When we need things, we go sometimes to one, sometimes the next, so people don't come to notice us much. And we sell where we can. But I guess we'll be moving on, one of these days. It's just about time."

It sounded rather sad to Winnie, never to belong anywhere. "That's too bad," she said, glancing shyly at Mae. "Always moving around and never having any friends or anything."

But Mae shrugged off this observation. "Tuck and me, we got each other," she said, "and that's a lot. The boys, now, they go their separate ways. They're some different, don't always get on too good. But they come home whenever the spirit moves, and every ten years, first week of August, they meet at the spring and come home *together* so's we can be a family again for a little while. That's why we was there this morning. One way or another, it all works out." She folded her arms and nodded, more to herself than to Winnie. "Life's got to be lived, no matter how long or short," she said calmly. "You got to take what comes. We just go along, like everybody else, one day at a time. Funny—we don't feel no different. Leastways, I don't. Sometimes I forget about what's happened to us, forget it altogether. And then sometimes it comes over me and I wonder why it happened to *us*. We're plain as salt, us Tucks. We don't deserve no blessings—if it is a blessing. And, likewise, I don't see how we deserve to be cursed, if it's a curse. Still—there's no use trying to figure why things fall the way they do. Things just are, and fussing don't bring changes. Tuck, now, he's got a few other ideas, but I expect he'll tell you. There! The boys are in from the pond."

Winnie heard a burst of voices downstairs, and in a moment Miles and Jesse were climbing to the loft.

"Here, child," said Mae hastily. "Hide your eyes. Boys? Are you decent? What'd you put on to swim in? I got Winnie up here, do you hear me?"

"For goodness' sake, Ma," said Jesse, emerging from the stairwell. "You think we're going to march around in our altogether with Winnie Foster in the house?"

And Miles, behind him, said, "We just jumped in with our clothes on. Too hot and tired to shed 'em."

It was true. They stood there side by side with their wet clothes plastered to their skins, little pools of water collecting at their feet.

"Well!" said Mae, relieved. "All right. Find something dry to put on. Your pa's got supper nearly ready." And she hustled Winnie down the narrow stairs.

11

It was a good supper, flapjacks, bacon, bread, and applesauce, but they ate sitting about in the parlor instead of around a table. Winnie had never had a meal that way before and she watched them carefully at first, to see what rules there might be that she did not know about. But there seemed to be no rules. Jesse sat on the floor and used the seat of a chair for a table, but the others held their plates in their laps. There were no napkins. It was all right, then, to lick the maple syrup from your fingers. Winnie was never allowed to do such a thing at home, but she had always thought it would be the easiest way. And suddenly the meal seemed luxurious.

After a few minutes, however, it was clear to Winnie that there was at least one rule: As long as there was food to eat, there was no conversation. All four

Tucks kept their eyes and their attention on the business at hand. And in the silence, given time to think, Winnie felt her elation, and her thoughtless pleasure, wobble and collapse.

It had been different when they were out-of-doors, where the world belonged to everyone and no one. Here, everything was theirs alone, everything was done their way. Eating, she realized now, was a very personal thing, not something to do with strangers. *Chewing* was a personal thing. Yet here she was, chewing with strangers in a strange place. She shivered a little, and frowned, looking round at them. That story they had told her—why, they were crazy, she thought harshly, and they were criminals. They had kidnapped her, right out of the middle of her very own wood, and now she would be expected to sleep —*all night*—in this dirty, peculiar house. She had never slept in any bed but her own in her life. All these thoughts flowed at once from the dark part of her mind. She put down her fork and said, unsteadily, "I want to go home."

The Tucks stopped eating, and looked at her, surprised. Mae said soothingly, "Why, of course you do, child. That's only natural. I'll take you home. I promised I would, soon's we've explained a bit as to why you got to promise you'll never tell about the spring. That's the only reason we brung you here. We got to make you see why."

Then Miles said, cheerfully and with sudden sympathy, "There's a pretty good old rowboat. I'll take you out for a row after supper."

"No, *I* will," said Jesse. "Let *me*. I found her first, didn't I, Winnie Foster? Listen, I'll show you where the frogs are, and . . ."

"Hush," Tuck interrupted. "Everyone hush. *I'll* take Winnie rowing on the pond. There's a good deal to be said and I think we better hurry up and say it. I got a feeling there ain't a whole lot of time."

Jesse laughed at this, and ran a hand roughly through his curls. "That's funny, Pa. Seems to me like time's the only thing we got a lot of."

But Mae frowned. "You worried, Tuck? What's got you? No one saw us on the way up. Well, now, wait a bit—yes, they did, come to think of it. There was a man on the road, just outside Treegap. But he didn't say nothing."

"He knows me, though," said Winnie. She had forgotten, too, about the man in the yellow suit, and now, thinking of him, she felt a surge of relief. "He'll tell my father he saw me."

"He knows you?" said Mae, her frown deepening. "But you didn't call out to him, child. Why not?"

"I was too scared to do *anything*," said Winnie honestly.

Tuck shook his head. "I never thought we'd come to the place where we'd be scaring children," he said. "I guess there's no way to make it up to you, Winnie, but I'm sure most awful sorry it had to happen like that. Who was this man you saw?"

"I don't know his name," said Winnie. "But he's a pretty nice man, I guess." In fact, he seemed supremely nice to her now, a kind of savior. And then she added, "He came to our house last night, but he didn't go inside."

"Well, that don't sound too serious, Pa," said Miles. "Just some stranger passing by."

"Just the same, we got to get you home again, Winnie," said Tuck, standing up decisively. "We got to get you home just as fast as we can. I got a feeling this whole thing is going to come apart like wet bread. But first we got to talk, and the pond's the best place. The pond's got answers. Come along, child. Let's go out on the water."

12

The sky was a ragged blaze of red and pink and orange, and its double trembled on the surface of the pond like color spilled from a paintbox. The sun was dropping fast now, a soft red sliding egg yolk, and already to the east there was a darkening to purple. Winnie, newly brave with her thoughts of being rescued, climbed boldly into the rowboat. The hard heels of her buttoned boots made a hollow banging sound against its wet boards, loud in the warm and breathless quiet. Across the pond a bullfrog spoke a deep note of warning. Tuck climbed in, too, pushing off, and, settling the oars into their locks, dipped them into the silty bottom in one strong pull. The rowboat slipped from the bank then, silently, and glided out, tall water grasses whispering away from its sides, releasing it.

Here and there the still surface of the water dimpled, and bright rings spread noiselessly and vanished. "Feeding time," said Tuck softly. And Winnie, looking down, saw hosts of tiny insects skittering and skating on the surface. "Best time of all for fishing," he said, "when they come up to feed."

He dragged on the oars. The rowboat slowed and began to drift gently toward the farthest end of the pond. It was so quiet that Winnie almost jumped when the bullfrog spoke again. And then, from the tall pines and birches that ringed the pond, a wood thrush caroled. The silver notes were pure and clear and lovely.

"Know what that is, all around us, Winnie?" said Tuck, his voice low. "Life. Moving, growing, changing, never the same two minutes together. This water, you look out at it every morning, and it *looks* the same, but it ain't. All night long it's been moving, coming in through the stream back there to the west, slipping out through the stream down east here, always quiet, always new, moving on. You can't hardly see the current, can you? And sometimes the wind makes it look like it's going the other way. But it's always there, the water's always moving on, and someday, after a long while, it comes to the ocean."

They drifted in silence for a time. The bullfrog spoke again, and from behind them, far back in some reedy, secret place, another bullfrog answered. In the fading light, the trees along the banks were slowly losing their dimensions, flattening into silhouettes clipped from black paper and pasted to the paling sky. The voice of a different frog, hoarser and not so deep, croaked from the nearest bank.

"Know what happens then?" said Tuck. "To the water? The sun sucks some of it up right out of the ocean and carries it back in clouds, and then it rains, and the rain falls into the stream, and the stream keeps moving on, taking it all back again. It's a wheel, Winnie. Everything's a wheel, turning and turning, never stopping. The frogs is part of it, and the bugs, and the fish, and the wood thrush, too. And people. But never the same ones. Always coming in new, always growing and changing, and always moving on. That's the way it's supposed to be. That's the way it *is*."

The rowboat had drifted at last to the end of the pond, but now its bow bumped into the rotting branches of a fallen tree that thrust thick fingers into the water. And though the current pulled at it, dragging its stern sidewise, the boat was wedged and could not follow. The water slipped past it, out between clumps of reeds and brambles, and gurgled down a narrow bed, over stones and pebbles, foaming a little, moving swiftly now after its slow trip between the pond's wide banks. And, farther down,

Winnie could see that it hurried into a curve, around a leaning willow, and disappeared.

"It goes on," Tuck repeated, "to the ocean. But this rowboat now, it's stuck. If we didn't move it out ourself, it would stay here forever, trying to get loose, but stuck. That's what us Tucks are, Winnie. Stuck so's we can't move on. We ain't part of the wheel no more. Dropped off, Winnie. Left behind. And everywhere around us, things is moving and growing and changing. You, for instance. A child now, but someday a woman. And after that, moving on to make room for the new children."

Winnie blinked, and all at once her mind was drowned with understanding of what he was saying. For she—yes, even she—would go out of the world willy-nilly someday. Just go out, like the flame of a candle, and no use protesting. It was a certainty. She would try very hard not to think of it, but sometimes, as now, it would be forced upon her. She raged against it, helpless and insulted, and blurted at last, "I don't want to die."

"No," said Tuck calmly. "Not now. Your time's not now. But dying's part of the wheel, right there next to being born. You can't pick out the pieces you like and leave the rest. Being part of the whole thing, that's the blessing. But it's passing us by, us Tucks. Living's heavy work, but off to one side, the way *we* are, it's useless, too. It don't make sense. If I knowed how to climb back on the wheel, I'd do it in a minute. You can't have living without dying. So you can't call it living, what we got. We just *are*, we just *be*, like rocks beside the road."

Tuck's voice was rough now, and Winnie, amazed, sat rigid. No one had ever talked to her of things like this before. "I want to grow again," he said fiercely, "and change. And if that means I got to move on at the end of it, then I want that, too. Listen, Winnie, it's something you don't find out how you feel until afterwards. If people knowed about the spring down there in Treegap, they'd all come running like pigs to slops. They'd trample each other, trying to get some of that water. That'd be bad enough, but afterwards—can you imagine? All the little ones little forever, all the old ones old forever. Can you picture what that means? *Forever*? The wheel would keep on going round, the water rolling by to the ocean, but the people would've turned into nothing but rocks by the side of the road. 'Cause they wouldn't know till after, and then it'd be too late." He peered at her, and Winnie saw that his face was pinched with the effort of explaining. "Do you see, now, child? Do you understand? Oh, Lord, I just got to make you understand!"

There was a long, long moment of silence. Winnie, struggling with the anguish of all these things, could only sit hunched and numb, the sound of the water rolling in her ears. It was black and silky now; it lapped at the sides of the rowboat and hurried on around them into the stream.

And then, down the length of the pond, a voice rang out. It was Miles, and every word, across the water, came clearly to their ears. "Pa! Pa, come back! Something's happened, Pa. The horse is gone. Can you hear me? Someone's stole the horse."

13

Sometime later, the man in the yellow suit slipped down from the saddle and tied the Tucks' old horse to a bar of the Fosters' fence. He tried the gate. It was unlocked. He pushed through and strode up the path to the door of the cottage. Though it was very late now, almost midnight, the windows glowed golden: the family had not gone to bed. The man in the yellow suit took off his hat and smoothed his hair with long white fingers. Then he knocked at the door. It was opened at once by Winnie's grandmother, and before she could speak, the man said quickly, "Ah! Good evening! May I come in? I have happy news for you. I know where they've taken the little girl."

14

There had been nothing for the Tucks to do but go to bed. It was too dark now to go out looking for the horse thief, and anyway, they had no idea when he had done his thieving or which way he had gone.

"That beats all, though, don't it, Pa," said Jesse, "coming up to a person's house and stealing their horse right out from under their nose!"

"I got to give you that," said Tuck. "But the question is, was it just some ordinary thief, or was it someone that had some special reason? I don't like it. I got a bad feeling about the whole thing."

"Hush now, Tuck," said Mae. She was spreading a quilt on the old sofa, making it into a bed for Winnie. "You're too much of a worrier. There's nothing we can do about it now, so there's no sense fussing. You got no reason to think there's anything peculiar about it, anyway. Come on, we'll get a good night's sleep and figure it out in the morning when we're fresh. Boys, up you go, and don't get talking—you'll keep us awake. Winnie, child, you bed down, too. You'll sleep first-rate on the sofa here."

But Winnie did not sleep at all, not for a long, long time. The cushions of the sofa were remarkably lumpy and smelled like old newspapers; and the chair pad Mae had given her for a pillow was thin and hard, and rough under her cheek. But far worse than this was the fact that she was still in her clothes, for she had firmly refused the offer of Mae's spare nightgown, with its seeming miles of faded cotton flannel. Only her own nightgown would do, and the regular bedtime routine; without them, she was painfully lonely for home. Her joy on the road that morning had completely disappeared; the wide world shrank and her oldest fears rolled freely in her consciousness. It was unbelievable that she should be in this place; it was an outrage. But she was helpless to do anything about it, helpless to control it, and exhausted by the conversation in the rowboat.

Was it true? Could they really never die, these Tucks? It had evidently not occurred to them that she might not believe it. They were only concerned that she keep the secret. Well, she did not believe it. It was nonsense. Wasn't it? Well, wasn't it?

Winnie's head whirled. Remembering the man in

the yellow suit was the only thing that kept her from weeping. "He's told them by now," she thought, rehearsing it. "They've been looking for me for hours. But they don't know where to look! No. The man saw which way we were headed. Papa will find me. They're out looking for me right now."

She went over it again and again, lying wrapped in the quilt, while outside the moon rose, turning the pond to silver. There was a hint of mist, now that the air was cooler, and the frogs talked comfortably. Crickets soon joined in with their shrill, rhythmic song. In the table drawer, the mouse rustled softly, enjoying the supper of flapjack crumbs Mae had put there for him. And at last these things were clearer in Winnie's ears than the voice of her thoughts. She began to relax, listening to the sound-filled silence. Then, just as she was drifting into sleep, she heard soft footsteps and Mae was beside her. "You resting easy, child?" she whispered.

"I'm all right, thank you," said Winnie.

"I'm sorry about everything," said Mae. "I just didn't know no other way but to bring you back with us. I know it ain't very happy for you here, but . . . well . . . anyway, you have a good talk with Tuck?"

"I guess so," said Winnie.

"That's good. Well. I'm going back to bed. Get a good sleep."

"All right," said Winnie.

But still Mae lingered. "We been alone so long," she said at last, "I guess we don't know how to do with visitors. But still and all, it's a good feeling, you being here with us. I wish you was . . . ours." She put out an awkward hand then and touched Winnie's hair. "Well," she said, "good night."

"Good night," said Winnie.

Tuck came, too, a little later, to peer down at her anxiously. He was wearing a long white nightshirt and his hair was rumpled. "Oh!" he said. "You still awake? Everything all right?"

"Yes," said Winnie.

"I didn't mean to go disturbing you," he said. "But I been laying in there thinking I ought to be setting out here with you till you went to sleep."

"You don't have to do that," said Winnie, surprised and touched. "I'm all right."

He looked uncertain. "Well . . . but if you want something, will you holler? I'm just in the next room —I'd be out here like a shot." And then he added, gruffly, "It's been quite a time since we had a natural, growing child in the house . . ." His voice trailed off. "Well. Try to get some sleep. That sofa there, I guess it ain't the kind of thing you're used to."

"It's fine," said Winnie.

"The bed's no better, or I'd switch with you," he said. He didn't seem to know how to finish the conversation. But then he bent and kissed her quickly on the cheek, and was gone.

Winnie lay with her eyes wide. She felt cared for and—confused. And all at once she wondered what would happen to the Tucks when her father came. What would he do to them? She would never be able to explain how they had been with her, how they made her feel. She remembered guiltily that at supper she had decided they were criminals. Well, but they *were*. And yet . . .

And then a final visitor made her confusion complete. There was a creaking on the loft stairs and Jesse was looking down at her, very beautiful and eager in the faint blue moonlight. "Hey, Winnie Foster," he whispered. "You asleep?"

This time she sat up, pulling the quilt around her in sudden embarrassment, and answered, "No, not yet."

"Well then, listen." He knelt beside her, his curls tumbled and his eyes wide. "I been thinking it over. Pa's right about you having to keep the secret. It's not hard to see why. But the thing is, you knowing about the water already, and living right next to it so's you could go there any time, well, listen, how'd it be if you was to wait till you're seventeen, same age as me—heck, that's only six years off—and then you could go and drink some, and then you could go away with me! We could get married, even. That'd be pretty good, wouldn't it! We could have a grand old time, go all around the world, see everything. Listen, Ma and Pa and Miles, they don't know how to enjoy it, what we got. Why, heck, Winnie, life's to enjoy yourself, isn't it? What else is it good for? That's what *I* say. And you and me, we could have a good time that never, never stopped. Wouldn't that be something?"

Once more Winnie adored him, kneeling there beside her in the moonlight. He wasn't crazy. How could he be? He was just—amazing. But she was struck dumb. All she could do was stare at him.

"You think on it, Winnie Foster," Jesse whispered earnestly. "Think on it some and see if it don't sound good. Anyway, I'll see you in the morning. All right?"

"All right," she managed to whisper in return. He slipped away then, back up the creaking steps, but Winnie sat upright, wide awake, her cheeks burning. She could not deal with this remarkable suggestion, she could not "think on it." For she didn't know what to believe about anything. She lay down again, finally, and stared into the moonlight for another half an hour before she fell asleep.

15

In Treegap, the same moonlight silvered the roof of the touch-me-not cottage, but inside, the lamps were burning. "That's right," said the man in the yellow suit. "I know where she is." He sat back in his chair in the Fosters' spotless parlor, crossing his long, thin legs, and the suspended foot began a rhythmic jiggling. He hung his hat on his knee and smiled, his eyes nearly closed. "I followed them, you see. She's with them now. As soon as I saw they'd arrived at their destination, I turned around and came directly back. I thought you'd be staying up. You've been looking for her all day, of course. It must be quite a worry."

He lifted a hand then, ignoring their exclamations, and began to smooth the thin hairs of his beard. "You know," he said thoughtfully, "I've come a long way, looking for a wood exactly like the one you've got next door here. It would mean a great deal to me to own it. And how pleasant to have neighbors like yourselves! Now, understand, I wouldn't cut down many of the trees. I'm no barbarian, you can see that. No, just a few. You wouldn't find it different at all, really." He gestured with his long, white fingers and smiled, his face crinkling pleasantly. "We'd be good friends, I think. Why, the little girl and I, we're friends already. It would be a great relief to see her safely home again, wouldn't it?" He clicked his tongue and frowned. "Dreadful thing, kidnapping. Isn't it fortunate that I was a witness! Why, without me, you might never have heard a word. They're rough country people, the ones that took her. There's just no telling what illiterates like that might do. Yes," he sighed, lifting his eyebrows and smiling again, "it looks as if I'm the only person in the whole world who knows where to find her."

And then the man in the yellow suit sat forward. His long face took on a hard expression. "Now, I don't have to spell things out for people like yourselves. Some types one comes across can't seem to cut their way through any problem, and that does make things difficult. But you, I don't have to explain the situation to *you*. I've got what you want, and you've got what I want. Of course, you might find that child without me, but . . . you might not find her in time.

So: I want the wood and you want the child. It's a trade. A simple, clear-cut trade."

He looked around at the three shocked faces, and as if he were seeing nothing there but calm agreement, he smiled delightedly and rubbed his hands together. "Done and done," he said. "I knew right away, I said to myself, 'Now here is a group of intelligent, reasonable people!' I'm seldom wrong as a judge of character. Very seldom disappointed. So! All that remains is to write it up on paper, giving me the wood, and to sign it. It's best, don't you agree, to keep things legal and tidy. The rest is easy. Nothing to it. You go for your local constable, and he and I ride out and bring back the child *and* the criminals. No—oh, no, Mr. Foster—I understand your concern, but you mustn't come along. We'll do this business my way. There now! Your terrible ordeal is as good as over, isn't it? I'm so thankful I was here to help you out!"

16

The constable was fat, and he was sleepy. He wheezed when he spoke. And he spoke quite a bit as they started off, he and the man in the yellow suit. "First they roust me out of bed in the middle of the night, after I been out since sun-up looking for that child, and now I s'pose you're going to try to run me all the way," he said sourly. "I got to tell you this horse of mine is none too strong. I don't have to hurry her as a rule, so most of the time it don't matter. Seems to me we could've waited till dawn, anyway."

The man in the yellow suit was as courteous as always. "The Fosters have been waiting since yesterday morning," he pointed out. "Naturally, they're very upset. The sooner we get there, the sooner that child will be with them again."

"How come *you're* so deep in it?" asked the constable suspiciously. "Maybe you're in cahoots with the kidnappers, how do I know? You should of reported it right off, when you saw her get snatched."

The man in the yellow suit sighed. "But of course I had to find out where they were taking her," he explained patiently. "I came right back after that. And the Fosters are friends of mine. They've—uh—sold me their wood."

The constable's eyes went round. "I'll be!" he said. "What do you know about that! I didn't suppose they'd ever do a thing like that, friend or no friend. They're the first family around here, you know. Proud as peacocks, all of 'em. Family-proud, and land-proud, too. But they sold off, did they? Well, well." And he whistled in amazement.

They thumped along in silence for a while, out around the wood and across the star-lit meadow. Then the constable yawned deeply and said, "You ready to tell me how long this is going to take? How far we got to go?"

"Twenty miles north," said the man in the yellow suit.

The constable groaned. "Twenty miles!" He shifted the shotgun that rested across his saddle, and groaned again. "Clear up in the foothills? That's a fair way, all right."

There was no reply to this. The constable ran his fingers down the gleaming barrel of the shotgun.

Then he shrugged, and slumped a little in the saddle. "Might as well relax," he wheezed, suddenly companionable. "We'll be riding three, four hours."

Still there was no reply.

"Yessir," said the constable, trying again. "It's something new for these parts, kidnapping. Never had a case like this before that I know of, and I been in charge going on fifteen years."

He waited.

"You don't say so," his companion said at last.

"Yep, that's a fact," said the constable, with evident relief. Maybe now there would be some conversation! "Yep, fifteen years. Seen a lot of trouble in fifteen years, but nothing quite like this. 'Course, there's a first time for everything, as they say. We got a brand-new jailhouse, did you notice? Listen, it's a dandy! Give those folks nice clean accommodations." He chuckled. " 'Course, they won't be there long. Circuit judge'll be coming through next week. He'll send 'em over to Charleyville, most likely, to the county jail. That's what they do for your serious crimes. 'Course, we got a gallows of our own, if we ever need it. Keeps down trouble, *I* think, just having it there. Ain't ever used it yet. That's because they take care of the serious stuff over to Charleyville, like I say."

The constable paused to light a cigar, and went on cheerfully: "What you got planned for that piece of Foster land? Going to clear her? Put up a house, or a store, maybe?"

"No," said the man in the yellow suit.

The constable waited for more, but there was no more. His sour mood returned. He frowned and shook the ashes from his cigar. "Say," he said. "You're kind of a close-lipped feller, ain't you?"

The man in the yellow suit narrowed his eyes. His mouth, above the thin gray beard, twitched with annoyance. "Look here," he said tightly. "Would you mind if I rode on ahead? I'm worried about that child. I'll tell you how to get there, and I'll go on ahead and keep watch."

"Well," said the constable grudgingly, "all right, if you're in such a ding-danged hurry. But don't do nothing till I get there. Those folks are likely dangerous. I'll try to keep up, but this horse of mine, she's none too strong. Don't see as how I could get her to a gallop, even if I tried."

"That's right," said the man in the yellow suit. "So I'll go on ahead, and wait outside the house till you get there."

He explained the route carefully, then dug his heels into the flanks of the fat old horse, cantering off into the darkness where just a hint of dawn glowed on the edges of the hills far ahead.

The constable chewed on the end of his cigar. "Humph," he said to his horse. "Did you get a gander at that suit of clothes? Oh, well, it takes all kinds, as they say." And he followed slowly after, yawning, the gap between him and the man ahead lengthening with every mile.

17

For the second morning in a row, Winnie Foster
woke early. Outside, in the ring of trees around the
pond, the birds were celebrating, giving the new
day a brass band's worth of greeting. Winnie freed
herself from the twisted quilt and went to a window.
Mist lay on the surface of the water, and the light
was still pale. It looked unreal, and she felt, herself,
unreal, waking where she had, with her hair wild
and her dress all crumpled. She rubbed her eyes.
Through the dewy weeds below the window, a toad
hopped suddenly into view and Winnie peered at it
eagerly. But no—of course it wasn't the same toad.
And remembering that other toad—*her* toad, she
thought now, almost fondly—it seemed to her that
she had been away from home for weeks. Then she

heard a step on the loft stairs and thought, "Jesse!"
At once her cheeks flamed.

But it was Miles. He came into the parlor, and
when he saw that she was up, he smiled and whispered, "Good! You're awake. Come on—you can
help me catch some fish for breakfast."

This time, Winnie was careful not to make a noise
when she climbed into the rowboat. She made her
way to her seat in the stern, and Miles handed her
two old cane poles—"Watch out for the hooks!" he
warned—and a jar of bait: pork fat cut into little
pieces. A big brown night moth fluttered out from
under the oar blades propped beside her on the seat,
and wobbled off toward nowhere through the fra-
grant air. And from the bank, something plopped
into the water. A frog! Winnie caught just a glimpse
of it as it scissored away from shore. The water was
so clear that she could see tiny brown fish near the
bottom, flicking this way and that.

Miles pushed the rowboat off and sprang in, and
soon they were gliding up toward the near end of
the pond, where the water came in from the stream.
The locks grated as the oars dipped and swung, but
Miles was skillful. He rowed without a single splash.
The dripping from the blades, as they lifted, sent
rows of overlapping circles spreading silently behind
them. It was very peaceful. "They'll take me home

today," thought Winnie. She was somehow certain of this, and began to feel quite cheerful. She had been kidnapped, but nothing bad had happened, and now it was almost over. Now, remembering the visits of the night before, she smiled—and found that she loved them, this most peculiar family. They were her friends, after all. And hers alone.

"How'd you sleep?" Miles asked her.

"All right," she said.

"That's good. I'm glad. Ever been fishing before?"

"No," she told him.

"You'll like it. It's fun." And he smiled at her.

The mist was lifting now, as the sun poked up above the trees, and the water sparkled. Miles guided the rowboat near a spot where lily pads lay like up-turned palms on the surface. "We'll let her drift some here," he said. "There'll be trout down in those weeds and stems. Here—give me the poles and I'll bait the hooks for us."

Winnie sat watching him as he worked. His face was like Jesse's, and yet not like. It was thinner, without Jesse's rounded cheeks, and paler, and his hair was almost straight, clipped neatly below the ears. His hands were different, too, the fingers thicker, the skin scrubbed-looking, but black at the knuckles and under the nails. Winnie remembered then that he worked sometimes as a blacksmith, and indeed his shoulders, under his threadbare shirt, were broad and muscled. He looked solid, like an oar, whereas Jesse—well, she decided, Jesse was like water: thin, and quick.

Miles seemed to sense that she was watching him. He looked up from the bait jar and his eyes, returning her gaze, were soft. "Remember I told you I had two children?" he asked. "Well, one of 'em was a girl. I took her fishing, too." His face clouded then, and he shook his head. "Her name was Anna. Lord, how sweet she was, that child! It's queer to think she'd be close to eighty now, if she's even still alive. And my son—he'd be eighty-two."

Winnie looked at his young, strong face, and after a moment she said, "Why didn't you take them to the spring and give them some of the special water?"

"Well, of course, we didn't realize about the spring while we was still on the farm," said Miles. "Afterwards, I thought about going to find them. I wanted to, heaven knows. But, Winnie, how'd it have been if I had? My wife was nearly forty by then. And the children—well, what was the use? They'd have been near growed theirselves. They'd have had a pa close to the same age *they* was. No, it'd all have been so mixed up and peculiar, it just wouldn't have worked. Then Pa, he was dead-set against it, anyway. The fewer people know about the spring, he says, the fewer there are to tell about it. Here—here's your pole. Just ease the hook down in the water. You'll know when you get a bite."

Winnie clutched her pole, sitting sidewise in the stern, and watched the baited hook sink slowly down. A dragonfly, a brilliant blue jewel, darted up and paused over the lily pads, then swung up and away. From the nearest bank, a bullfrog spoke.

"There certainly are a lot of frogs around here," Winnie observed.

"That's so," said Miles. "They'll keep coming, too, long as the turtles stay away. Snappers, now, they'll eat a frog soon as look at him."

Winnie thought about this peril to the frogs, and sighed. "It'd be nice," she said, "if nothing ever had to die."

"Well, now, I don't know," said Miles. "If you think on it, you come to see there'd be so many creatures, including people, we'd all be squeezed in right up next to each other before long."

Winnie squinted at her fishing line and tried to picture a teeming world. "Mmm," she said, "yes, I guess you're right."

Suddenly the cane pole jerked in her hands and bent into an arch, its tip dragged down nearly to the water's surface. Winnie held on tight to the handle, her eyes wide.

"Hey!" cried Miles. "Look there! You got a bite. Fresh trout for breakfast, Winnie."

But just as suddenly the pole whipped straight again and the line went slack. "Shucks," said Miles. "It got away."

"I'm kind of glad," Winnie admitted, easing her rigid grip on the butt of the pole. "*You* fish, Miles. I'm not so sure I want to."

And so they drifted for a little longer. The sky was blue and hard now, the last of the mist dissolved, and the sun, stepping higher above the trees, was hot on Winnie's back. The first week of August was reasserting itself after a good night's sleep. It would be another searing day.

A mosquito appeared and sat down on Winnie's knee. She slapped at it absently, thinking about what Miles had said. If all the mosquitoes lived forever—and if they kept on having babies!—it would be terrible. The Tucks were right. It was best if no one knew about the spring, including the mosquitoes. She would keep the secret. She looked at Miles, and then she asked him, "What will you do, if you've got so much time?"

"Someday," said Miles, "I'll find a way to do something important."

Winnie nodded. That was what *she* wanted.

"The way I see it," Miles went on, "it's no good hiding yourself away, like Pa and lots of other people. And it's no good just thinking of your own pleasure, either. People got to do something useful if they're going to take up space in the world."

"But what will you *do?*" Winnie persisted.

"I don't know yet," said Miles. "I ain't had no schooling or nothing, and that makes it harder." Then he set his jaw and added, "I'll find a way, though. I'll locate something."

Winnie nodded. She reached out and ran her fingers across a lily pad that lay on the water beside the boat. It was warm and very dry, like a blotter, but near its center was a single drop of water, round and perfect. She touched the drop and brought her fingertip back wet; but the drop of water, though it rolled a little, remained as round and perfect as before.

And then Miles caught a fish. There it flopped, in the bottom of the boat, its jaw working, its gills fanning rapidly. Winnie drew up her knees and stared at it. It was beautiful, and horrible too, with gleaming, rainbow-colored scales, and an eye like a marble beginning to dim even as she watched it. The hook was caught in its upper lip, and suddenly Winnie wanted to weep. "Put it back, Miles," she said, her voice dry and harsh. "Put it back right away."

Miles started to protest, and then, looking at her face, he picked up the trout and gently worked the barbed hook free. "All right, Winnie," he said. He dropped the fish over the edge of the boat. It flipped its tail and disappeared under the lily pads.

"Will it be all right?" asked Winnie, feeling foolish and happy both at once.

"It'll be all right," Miles assured her. And then he said, "People got to be meat-eaters sometimes, though. It's the natural way. And that means killing things."

"I know," said Winnie weakly. "But still."

"Yes," said Miles. "I know."

18

And so there were flapjacks again for breakfast, but no one seemed to mind. "Didn't get a bite, eh?" said Mae.

"No," said Miles, "nothing we wanted to keep."

That was true, anyway. And though Winnie blushed as he said it, she was grateful that he didn't explain.

"Never mind," said Mae. "You're likely out of practice. Tomorrow, maybe."

"Sure," said Miles. "Tomorrow."

But it was the thought of seeing Jesse again that kept Winnie's stomach fluttering. And at last he came down from the loft, yawning and rosy, rubbing his curls, just as Mae was piling the plates with flapjacks. "Well, slug-a-bed," she said to him fondly. "You come near to missing breakfast. Miles and Winnie been up for hours, out fishing and back already."

"Oh?" said Jesse, his eyes on Miles. "Where's the fish, then? How come we got nothing but flapjacks?"

"No luck," said Mae. "They wasn't biting, for some reason."

"Reason is, Miles don't know how to fish," said Jesse. He grinned at Winnie and she lowered her eyes, her heart thumping.

"It don't matter," said Mae. "We got plenty without. Come and get your plates, everybody."

They sat about in the parlor, as they had the night before. The ceiling swam with bright reflections, and sunlight streamed across the dusty, chip-strewn floor. Mae surveyed it all and sighed contentedly. "Now, this is real nice," she said, her fork poised above her plate. "Everyone sitting down together. And having Winnie here—why, it's just like a party."

"That's the truth," said Jesse and Miles both together, and Winnie felt a rush of happiness.

"Still, we got things to discuss," Tuck reminded them. "There's the business of the horse getting stole. And we got to get Winnie home where she belongs. How we going to do that without the horse?"

"After breakfast, Tuck," said Mae firmly. "Don't spoil a good meal with a lot of talk. We'll get to it soon enough."

So they were silent, eating, and this time Winnie

licked the syrup from her fingers without pausing to think about it first. Her fears at last night's supper seemed silly to her now. Perhaps they *were* crazy, but they weren't criminals. She loved them. They belonged to her.

Tuck said, "How'd you sleep, child?"

And she answered, "Just fine," and wished, for a fleeting moment, that she could stay with them forever in that sunny, untidy little house by the pond. Grow up with them and perhaps, if it was true about the spring—then perhaps, when she was seventeen . . . She glanced at Jesse, where he sat on the floor, his curly head bent over his plate. Then she looked at Miles. And then her eyes went to Tuck and lingered on his sad, creased face. It occurred to her that he was the dearest of them all, though she couldn't have explained why she felt that way.

However, there wasn't time to wonder, for at that moment someone knocked at the door.

It was such an alien sound, so sudden and surprising, that Mae dropped her fork, and everyone looked up, startled. "Who's that?" said Tuck.

"I can't imagine," whispered Mae. "We ain't never had callers in all the years we been here."

The knock came again.

"I'll go, Ma," said Miles.

"No, stay where you are," she said. "*I'll* go." She

put her plate down carefully on the floor and stood up, straightening her skirts. Then she went to the kitchen and opened the door.

Winnie recognized the voice at once. It was a rich and pleasant voice. The man in the yellow suit. And he was saying, "Good morning, Mrs. Tuck. It *is* Mrs. Tuck, isn't it. May I come in?"

19

The man in the yellow suit came into the sunlit parlor. He stood for a moment, looking around at them all, Mae and Miles and Jesse and Tuck, and Winnie, too. His face was without expression, but there was something unpleasant behind it that Winnie sensed at once, something that made her instantly suspicious. And yet his voice was mild when he said, "You're safe now, Winifred. I've come to take you home."

"We was going to bring her back directly, ourself," said Tuck, standing up slowly. "She ain't been in no danger."

"You're Mr. Tuck, I suppose," said the man in the yellow suit.

"I am," said Tuck formally, his back straighter than usual.

"Well, you may as well sit down again. You, too, Mrs. Tuck. I have a great deal to say and very little time for saying it."

Mae sat down on the edge of the rocker, and Tuck sat, too, but his eyes were narrowed.

Jesse said, uneasily, "Who in tarnation do you think you—"

But Tuck interrupted. "Hush, boy. Let him speak his piece."

"That's wise," said the man in the yellow suit. "I'll be as brief as possible." He took off his hat and laid it on the mantel, and then he stood tapping his foot on the littered hearth, facing them. His face was smooth and empty. "I was born west of here," he began, "and all the time I was growing up, my grandmother told me stories. They were wild, unbelievable stories, but *I* believed them. They involved a dear friend of my grandmother's who married into a very odd family. Married the older of two sons, and they had two children. It was after the children were born that she began to see that the family was odd. This friend of my grandmother's, she lived with her husband for twenty years, and strange to say, he never got any older. *She* did, but he didn't. And neither did his mother or his father or his brother. People began to wonder about that family, and my grandmother's friend decided at last that they were witches, or worse. She left her husband and came with her children to live at my grandmother's house for a short while. Then she moved west. I don't know what became of her. But my mother still remembers playing with the children. They were all about the same age. There was a son, and a daughter."

"Anna!" whispered Miles.

Mae burst out, "You got no call to come and bring us pain!"

And Tuck added roughly, "You got something to say, you better come to the point and say it."

"There, there, now," said the man in the yellow suit. He spread his long, white fingers in a soothing gesture. "Hear me out. As I've told you, I was fascinated by my grandmother's stories. People who never grew older! It was fantastic. It took possession of me. I decided to devote my life to finding out if it could be true, and if so, how and why. I went to school, I went to a university, I studied philosophy, metaphysics, even a little medicine. None of it did me any good. Oh, there were ancient legends, but nothing more. I nearly gave it up. It began to seem ridiculous, and a waste of time. I went home. My grandmother was very old by then. I took her a present one day, a music box. And when I gave it to her, it reminded her of something: the woman, the mother of the family that didn't grow old, *she* had had a music box."

Mae's hand went to the pocket of her skirt. Her

mouth opened, and then she shut it again with a snap.

"That music box played a very particular tune," the man in the yellow suit went on. "My grandmother's friend and her children—Anna? Was that the daughter's name?—they'd heard it so often that they knew it by heart. They'd taught it to my mother during the short time they lived in the house. We talked about it then, all those years afterward, my mother, my grandmother, and I. My mother was able to remember the melody, finally. She taught it to me. That was nearly twenty years ago now, but I kept it in my head. It was a clue."

The man in the yellow suit folded his arms and rocked a little. His voice was easy, almost friendly. "During those twenty years," he said, "I worked at other things. But I couldn't forget the tune or the family that didn't grow older. They haunted my dreams. So a few months ago I left my home and I started out to look for them, following the route they were said to have taken when they left their farm. No one I asked along the way knew anything. No one had heard of them, no one recognized their name. But two evenings ago, I heard that music box, I heard that very tune, and it was coming from the Fosters' wood. And next morning early, I saw the family at last, taking Winifred away. I followed, and I heard their story, every word."

Mae's face drained of color. Her mouth hung open. And Tuck said hoarsely, "What you going to do?"

The man in the yellow suit smiled. "The Fosters have given me the wood," he said. "In exchange for bringing Winifred home. I was the only one who knew where she was, you see. So it was a trade. Yes, I followed you, Mrs. Tuck, and then I took your horse and went directly back."

The tension in the parlor was immense. Winnie found that she could scarcely breathe. It *was* true, then! Or was the man who stood there crazy, too?

"Horse thief!" cried Tuck. "Get to the point! What you going to do?"

"It's very simple," said the man in the yellow suit. And, as he said this, the smoothness of his face began to loosen a little. A faint flush crept up his neck, and the pitch of his voice lifted, became a fraction higher. "Like all magnificent things, it's very simple. The wood—and the spring—belong to me now." He patted his breast pocket. "I have a paper here, all signed and legal, to prove it. I'm going to sell the water, you see."

"You can't do that!" roared Tuck. "You got to be out of your mind!"

The man in the yellow suit frowned. "But I'm not going to sell it to just anybody," he protested. "Only to certain people, people who deserve it. And it will be very, very expensive. But who wouldn't give a fortune to live forever?"

"I wouldn't," said Tuck grimly.

"Exactly," said the man in the yellow suit. His eyes glowed. "Ignorant people like you should never have the opportunity. It should be kept for . . . certain others. And for me. However, since it's already too late to keep you out, you may as well join me in what I'm going to do. You can show me where the spring is and help me to advertise. We'll set up demonstrations. You know—things that would be fatal to anybody else, but won't affect you in the least. I'll pay for your assistance, of course. It won't take long for the word to spread. And then you can go your way. Well, what do you say?"

Jesse said dully, "Freaks. You want us to be freaks. In a patent-medicine show."

The man in the yellow suit raised his eyebrows and a nervous petulance came into his voice. "Of course, if the idea doesn't appeal to you," he said, blinking rapidly, "you needn't be in on it. I can find the spring and manage just as well without you. But it seemed the gentlemanly thing to make the offer. After all," he added, looking round at the cluttered room, "it would mean you could afford to live like people again, instead of pigs."

And that was when the tension burst. All four Tucks sprang to their feet at once, while Winnie, very frightened, shrank back in her chair. Tuck cried, "You're a madman! A loony! You can't let *no* one know about that water. Don't you see what would *happen*?"

"I've given you your chance," shrilled the man in the yellow suit, "and you've refused it." He seized Winnie roughly by the arm and dragged her up out of her chair. "I'll take the child, and be on about my business."

Tuck began to rave now, his face stretched with horror. "Madman!" he shouted. And Miles and Jesse began to shout, too. They crowded after as the man in the yellow suit dragged Winnie through the kitchen to the door.

"No!" she was screaming, for now at last she hated him. "I won't go with you! I won't!"

But he opened the door and pushed her out in front of him. His eyes were like blind firepoints, his face was twisted.

Then the shouting behind them stopped abruptly, and in the midst of the sudden silence came Mae's voice, flat and cold. "You leave that child be," she said.

Winnie stared. Mae was standing just outside the doorway. She held Tuck's long-forgotten shotgun by the barrel, like a club.

The man in the yellow suit smiled a ghastly smile. "I can't think why you're so upset. Did you really believe you could keep that water for yourselves? Your selfishness is really quite extraordinary, and worse than that, you're stupid. You could have done what I'm about to do, long ago. Now it's too late. Once Winifred drinks some of the water, she'll do just as well for my demonstrations. Even better. Children are much more appealing, anyway. So you may as well relax. There's nothing you can do to stop me."

But he was wrong. Mae lifted the shotgun. Behind her, Miles gasped, "Ma! *No!*"

But Mae's face was dark red. "Not Winnie!" she said between clenched teeth. "You ain't going to do a thing like that to Winnie. And you ain't going to give out the secret." Her strong arms swung the shotgun round her head, like a wheel. The man in the yellow suit jerked away, but it was too late. With a dull cracking sound, the stock of the shotgun smashed into the back of his skull. He dropped like a tree, his face surprised, his eyes wide open. And at that very moment, riding through the pine trees just in time to see it all, came the Treegap constable.

20

Winnie was standing with her cheek pressed into Tuck's chest, her arms flung tight around him. She trembled, and kept her eyes squeezed shut. She could feel Tuck's breath come and go in little gasps. It was very quiet.

The Treegap constable knelt over the sprawled body of the man in the yellow suit, and then he said, "He ain't dead. Leastways, not yet."

Winnie opened her eyes a crack. She could see the shotgun lying on the grass where Mae had dropped it. She could see Mae's hands, too, hanging limp, clenching, then hanging limp again. The sun was scorching hot, and near her ear a gnat whined.

The constable stood up. "What did you hit him for?" he wheezed resentfully.

"He was taking the child away," said Mae. Her

voice was dull and exhausted. "He was taking the child against her will."

At this the constable exploded. "Ding-dang it, woman, what you trying to say? Taking that child against her will? That's what *you* done. You *kidnapped* that child."

Winnie let go of Tuck's waist and turned around. Her trembling had stopped. "They didn't kidnap me," she said. "I came because I wanted to."

Behind her, Tuck drew his breath in sharply.

"You wanted to?" echoed the constable, his eyes wide with disbelief. "You *wanted* to?"

"That's right," said Winnie unflinchingly. "They're my friends."

The constable stared at her. He scratched his chin, eyebrows high, and eased his own shotgun to the ground. Then he shrugged and looked down at the man in the yellow suit, who lay motionless on the grass, the blazing sun white on his face and hands. His eyes were closed now, but except for that, he looked more than ever like a marionette, a marionette flung carelessly into a corner, arms and legs every which way midst tangled strings.

The one glance she gave him fixed his appearance forever in Winnie's mind. She turned her eyes away quickly, looking to Tuck for relief. But Tuck was not looking back at her. Instead, he was gazing at the body on the ground, leaning forward slightly, his brows drawn down, his mouth a little open. It was as if he were entranced and—yes, envious—like a starving man looking through a window at a banquet. Winnie could not bear to see him like that. She reached out a hand and touched him, and it broke the spell. He blinked and took her hand, squeezing it.

"Well, anyway," said the constable at last, turning businesslike, "I got to take charge here. Get this feller into the house before he fries. I'm telling you now: if he don't make it, you're in a pickle, you people. Now, here's what we'll do. You," he said, pointing at Mae, "you got to come with me, you and the little girl. You got to be locked up right away; and the little girl, I got to get her home. The rest of you, you stay here with him. Look after him. I'll get back with a doctor quick as I can. Should have brought a deputy, but I didn't expect nothing like this to happen. Well, it's too late now. All right, let's get moving."

Miles said softly, "Ma. We'll get you out right away."

"Sure, Ma," said Jesse.

"Don't worry about me none," said Mae in the same exhausted voice. "I'll make out."

"Make out?" exclaimed the constable. "You people beat all. If this feller dies, you'll get the gallows, that's what you'll get, if that's what you mean by make out."

Tuck's face crumpled. "The gallows?" he whispered. "Hanging?"

"That's it," said the constable. "That's the law. Now, let's get going."

Miles and Jesse lifted the man in the yellow suit and carried him carefully into the house, but Tuck stood staring, and Winnie could guess what he was thinking. The constable swung her up onto his horse and directed Mae to her own saddle. But Winnie kept her eyes on Tuck. His face was very pale, the creases deeper than ever, and his eyes looked blank and sunken. She heard him whisper again, "The gallows!"

And then Winnie said something she had never said before, but the words were words she had sometimes heard, and often longed to hear. They sounded strange on her own lips and made her sit up straighter. "Mr. Tuck," she said, "don't worry. Everything's going to be all right."

The constable glanced heavenward and shook his head. Then, clutching his shotgun, he climbed up behind Winnie and turned the horse toward the path. "You first," he barked at Mae. "I got to keep an eye on you. And as for you," he added grimly, speaking to Tuck, "you better hope that feller don't die on you. I'll be back soon as I can."

"Everything'll be all right," Tuck repeated slowly.

Mae, slumped on the back of the fat old horse, did

not respond. But Winnie leaned round the constable and looked back at Tuck. "You'll see," she said. And then she faced forward, sitting very straight. She was going home, but the thought of that was far from her mind. She watched the rump of the horse ahead, the swish of coarse, dusty hairs as he moved his tail. And she watched the swaying, sagging back of the woman who rode him.

Up through the dim pine trees they went, the constable's breath wheezing in her ears, and emerging from the coolness and the green, Winnie saw again the wide world spread before her, shimmering with light and possibility. But the possibilities were different now. They did not point to what might happen to her but to what she herself might keep from happening. For the only thing she could think of was the clear and terrible necessity: Mae Tuck must never go to the gallows. Whatever happened to the man in the yellow suit, Mae Tuck must not be hanged. Because if all they had said was true, then Mae, even if she were the cruelest of murderers and deserved to be put to death—Mae Tuck would not be able to die.

21

Winnie pulled her little rocking chair up to her bedroom window and sat down. The rocking chair had been given to her when she was very small, but she still squeezed into it sometimes, when no one was looking, because the rocking made her almost remember something pleasant, something soothing, that would never quite come up to the surface of her mind. And tonight she wanted to be soothed.

The constable had brought her home. They had seized her at once, flinging the gate open and swooping down on her, her mother weeping, her father speechless, hugging her to him, her grandmother babbling with excitement. There was a painful pause when the constable told them she had gone away of her own free will, but it only lasted for a moment. They did not, would not believe it, and her grandmother said, "It was the elves. We heard them. They must have bewitched her."

And so they had borne her into the house, and after she had taken the bath they insisted upon, they fed and petted her and refused, with little laughs and murmurs, to accept her answers to their questions: She had gone away with the Tucks because—well, she just wanted to. The Tucks had been very kind to her, had given her flapjacks, taken her fishing. The Tucks were good and gentle people. All this would have been swept away in any case, however, this good impression of her friends which she was trying to create, when she told them what had happened to the man in the yellow suit. Had they really given him the wood in exchange for finding her? They had. Well, perhaps he wouldn't want it now. Mae had hit him with the shotgun. He was very sick. They received this news with mingled hope and horror, and her father said, "I suppose the wood will be ours again if that man should . . . that is, if he doesn't . . ."

"You mean, if he dies," Winnie had said, flatly, and they had sat back, shocked. Soon after, they put her to bed, with many kisses. But they peered at her anxiously over their shoulders as they tiptoed out of her bedroom, as if they sensed that she was different now from what she had been before. As if some part of her had slipped away.

Well, thought Winnie, crossing her arms on the windowsill, she *was* different. Things had happened to her that were hers alone, and had nothing to do with them. It was the first time. And no amount of telling about it could help them understand or share what she felt. It was satisfying and lonely, both at once. She rocked, gazing out at the twilight, and the soothing feeling came reliably into her bones. That feeling—it tied her to them, to her mother, her father, her grandmother, with strong threads too ancient and precious to be broken. But there were new threads now, tugging and insistent, which tied her just as firmly to the Tucks.

Winnie watched the sky slide into blackness over the wood outside her window. There was not the least hint of a breeze to soften the heavy August night. And then, over the treetops, on the faraway horizon, there was a flash of white. Heat lightning. Again and again it throbbed, without a sound. It was like pain, she thought. And suddenly she longed for a thunderstorm.

She cradled her head in her arms and closed her eyes. At once the image of the man in the yellow suit rose up. She could see him again, sprawled motionless on the sun-blanched grass. "He can't die," she whispered, thinking of Mae. "He mustn't." And then she considered his plans for the water in the spring, and Tuck's voice saying, "They'd all come running like pigs to slops." And she found herself thinking, "If it's true about the spring, then he has to die. He must. And that's why she did it."

Then she heard hoofbeats on the road below, a horse hurrying into the village, and not long after, there were footsteps and a knocking on the door. Winnie crept out of her room and crouched in the shadows at the top of the stairs. It was the constable. She heard him saying, "So that's that, Mr. Foster. We can't press no kidnapping charges, since your little girl claims there *wasn't* no kidnapping. But it don't matter now, anyway. The doc just got back a few minutes ago. That feller—the one you sold your land to? He's dead." There was a pause, and the murmur of other voices; then a match striking, the acrid smell of fresh cigar smoke. "Yep, she got him a good one, all right. He never even come to. So it's an open-and-shut case, since I seen her do it. Eyewitness. No question about it. They'll hang her for sure."

Winnie went back to her room and climbed into bed. She lay in the dark, propped up on the pillows, and stared at the lighter square of her window, at the heat lightning throbbing. It was like pain, she thought again, a dull pain on the fringes of the sky. Mae had killed the man in the yellow suit. And she had meant to kill him.

Winnie had killed a wasp once, in fear and anger, just in time to spare herself a stinging. She had slammed at the wasp with a heavy book, and killed it. And then, seeing its body broken, the thin wings stilled, she had wished it were alive again. She had wept for that wasp. Was Mae weeping now for the man in the yellow suit? In spite of her wish to spare the world, did she wish he were alive again? There was no way of knowing. But Mae had done what she thought she had to do. Winnie closed her eyes to shut out the silent pulsing of the lightning. Now *she* would have to do something. She had no idea what, but something. Mae Tuck must not go to the gallows.

22

Next morning Winnie went out to the fence directly after breakfast. It was the hottest day yet, so heavy that the slightest exertion brought on a flood of perspiration, an exhaustion in the joints. Two days before, they would have insisted that she stay indoors, but now, this morning, they were careful with her, a little gingerly, as if she were an egg. She had said, "I'm going outside now," and they had said, "All right, but come in if it gets too hot, won't you, dear?" And she had answered, "Yes."

The earth, where it was worn bald under the gate, was cracked, and hard as rock, a lifeless tan color; and the road was an aisle of brilliant velvet dust. Winnie leaned against the fence, her hands gripping the warm metal of the bars, and thought about Mae behind another set of bars in the jailhouse. And then, lifting her head, she saw the toad. It was squatting where she had seen it first, across the road. "Hello!" she said, very glad to see it.

The toad did not so much as flick a muscle or blink an eye. It looked dried out today, parched. "It's thirsty," said Winnie to herself. "No wonder, on a day like this." She left the fence and went back into the cottage. "Granny, can I have some water in a dish? There's a toad out front that looks as if he's just about to die of thirst."

"A toad?" said her grandmother, wrinkling her nose in disgust. "Nasty things, toads."

"Not this one," said Winnie. "This one is always out there, and I like him. Can I give him a drink of water?"

"Toads don't drink water, Winifred. It wouldn't do him any good."

"They don't drink water at all?"

"No. They take it in through their skins, like a sponge. When it rains."

"But it hasn't rained forever!" said Winnie, alarmed. "I could sprinkle some water on him, couldn't I? That would help, wouldn't it?"

"Well, I suppose so," said her grandmother. "Where is he? In the yard?"

"No," said Winnie. "He's across the road."

"I'll come with you, then. I don't want you leaving the yard alone."

But when they came out to the fence, Winnie balancing a small bowl of water with enormous care, the toad was gone.

"Well, he must be all right," said her grandmother. "If he could hop off."

With mingled disappointment and relief, Winnie tipped the water onto the cracked earth at the gate. It was sucked in immediately, and the wet brown stain it left behind paled and vanished almost as quickly.

"I never saw such heat in all my life," said Winnie's grandmother, dabbing uselessly at her neck with a handkerchief. "Don't stay out here much longer."

"I won't," said Winnie, and was left alone once more. She sat down on the grass and sighed. Mae! What could she do to set Mae free? She closed her eyes against the glaring light, and watched, a little dizzily, as brilliant patterns of red and orange danced inside her eyelids.

And then, miraculously, Jesse was there, crouching just on the other side of the fence. "Winnie!" he hissed. "You sleeping?"

"Oh, Jesse!" Her eyes flew open and she reached through the fence to grasp his hand. "I'm so glad to see you! What can we do? We have to get her out!"

"Miles's got a plan, but I don't see how it can work," said Jesse, speaking quickly, his voice almost a whisper. "He knows a lot about carpentering. He says he can take Ma's window frame right straight out of the wall, bars and all, and she can climb through. We're going to try it tonight when it gets dark. Only trouble is, that constable keeps watching her every minute, he's so durned proud of having a prisoner in that new jail of his. We been down to see her. She's all right. But even if she can climb through the window, he'll come after her soon's he sees she's gone. Seems to me he'll notice right off. That don't give us much time to get away. But we got to try it. There ain't no other way. Anyhow, I come to say goodbye. We won't be able to come back here for a long, long time, Winnie, if we get away. I mean, they'll be looking for Ma. Winnie, listen—I won't see you again, not for ages. Look now—here's a bottle of water from the spring. You keep it. And then, no matter where you are, when you're seventeen, Winnie, you can drink it, and then come find us. We'll leave directions somehow. Winnie, please say you will!"

He pressed the little bottle into her hands and Winnie took it, closing her fingers over it. "Jesse, wait!" she whispered breathlessly, for all at once she had the answer. "I can help! When your mother climbs out the window, I'll climb in and take her place. I can wrap myself up in her blanket, and when the constable looks in, he won't be able to tell the difference. Not in the dark. I can hump up and look a lot bigger. Miles can even put the window back.

That would give you time to get away! You'd have at least till morning!"

Jesse squinted at her, and then he said, "Yep—you know, it might work. It might just make the difference. But I don't know as Pa's going to want you taking any risk. I mean, what'll they say to you after, when they find out?"

"I don't know," said Winnie, "but it doesn't matter. Tell your father I want to help. I *have* to help. If it wasn't for me, there wouldn't have been any trouble in the first place. Tell him I have to."

"Well . . . all right. Can you get out after dark?"

"Yes," said Winnie.

"Then—at midnight, Winnie. I'll be waiting for you right here at midnight."

"Winifred!" an anxious voice called from the cottage. "Who's that you're talking to?"

Winnie stood up and turned to answer. "It's just a boy, Granny. I'll be in in a minute." When she turned around again, Jesse was gone. Winnie clutched the little bottle in her hands and tried to control the rising excitement that made her breath catch. At midnight she would make a difference in the world.

23

It was the longest day: mindlessly hot, unspeakably hot, too hot to move or even think. The countryside, the village of Treegap, the wood—all lay defeated. Nothing stirred. The sun was a ponderous circle without edges, a roar without a sound, a blazing glare so thorough and remorseless that even in the Fosters' parlor, with curtains drawn, it seemed an actual presence. You could not shut it out.

Winnie's mother and grandmother sat plaintive all afternoon in the parlor, fanning themselves and sipping lemonade, their hair unsettled and their knees loose. It was totally unlike them, this lapse from gentility, and it made them much more interesting. But Winnie didn't stay with them. Instead, she took her own brimming glass to her room and sat in her little rocker by the window. Once she had hidden Jesse's bottle in a bureau drawer, there was nothing to do but wait. In the hall outside her room, the grandfather's clock ticked deliberately, unimpressed with anyone's impatience, and Winnie found herself rocking to its rhythm—forward, back, forward, back, tick, tock, tick, tock. She tried to read, but it was so quiet that she could not concentrate, and so she was glad when at last it was time for supper. It was something to do, though none of them could manage more than a nibble.

But later, when Winnie went out again to the fence, she saw that the sky was changing. It was not so much clouding up as thickening, somehow, from every direction at once, the blank blue gone to haze. And then, as the sun sank reluctantly behind the treetops, the haze hardened to a brilliant brownish-yellow. In the wood, the leaves turned underside-up, giving the trees a silvery cast.

The air was noticeably heavier. It pressed on Winnie's chest and made her breathing difficult. She turned and went back into the cottage. "It's going to rain, I think," she told the prostrate group in the parlor, and the news was received with little moans of gratitude.

Everyone went to bed early, closing windows firmly on their way. For outside, though it was almost dark, shreds of the hard brown-yellow light lingered on the rims of things, and there was a wind beginning, small gusts that rattled the fence gate and set the trees to rustling. The smell of rain hung sweet in the air. "What a week *this* has been!" said Winnie's grandmother. "Well, thank the Lord, it's almost over." And Winnie thought to herself: Yes, it's almost over.

There were three hours to wait before midnight and nothing whatever to do. Winnie wandered restlessly about her room, sat in her rocker, lay on her bed, counted the ticks of the hall clock. Beneath her excitement, she was thick with guilt. For the second time in three short days—though they seemed many more than that—she was about to do something which she knew would be forbidden. She didn't have to ask.

Winnie had her own strong sense of rightness. She knew that she could always say, afterward, "Well, you never told me *not* to!" But how silly that would be! Of course it would never occur to them to include such a thing on their list of don'ts. She could hear them saying it, and almost smiled: "Now, remember, Winifred—don't bite your fingernails, don't interrupt when someone else is speaking, and don't go down to the jailhouse at midnight to change places with prisoners."

Still, it wasn't really funny. What would happen in the morning, when the constable found her in the cell and had to bring her home for the second time? What would they say? Would they ever trust her again? Winnie squirmed, sitting in the rocker, and swallowed uncomfortably. Well, she would have to make them understand, somehow, without explaining.

The hall clock chimed eleven. Outside, the wind had stopped. Everything, it seemed, was waiting. Winnie lay down and closed her eyes. Thinking of Tuck and Mae, of Miles and Jesse, her heart softened. They needed her. To take care of them. For in the funny sort of way that had struck her at the first, they were helpless. Or too trusting. Well, *something* like that. Anyway, they needed her. She would not disappoint them. Mae would go free. No one would have to find out—Winnie would not have to find out—that Mae could not . . . but Winnie blocked the picture from her mind, the horror that would prove the secret. Instead, she turned her thoughts to Jesse. When she was seventeen—would she? If it was true, would she? And if she did, would she be sorry afterwards? Tuck had said, "It's something you don't find out how you feel until afterwards." But no—it wasn't true. She knew that, now, here in her own bedroom. They were probably crazy after all. But she loved them anyway. They needed her. And, thinking this, Winnie fell asleep.

She woke with a jerk sometime later, and sat up,

alarmed. The clock was ticking steadily, the darkness was complete. Outside, the night seemed poised on tiptoe, waiting, waiting, holding its breath for the storm. Winnie stole out to the hall and frowned at the clock face in the shadows. And at last she could make it out, for the black Roman numerals were just barely visible against their white ground, the brass hands glowed faintly. As she peered at them, the long hand snapped forward one more notch, with a loud click. She had not missed her moment—it was five minutes to midnight.

24

Leaving the house was so easy that Winnie felt faintly shocked. She had half expected that the instant she put a foot on the stairs they would leap from their beds and surround her with accusations. But no one stirred. And she was struck by the realization that, if she chose, she could slip out night after night without their knowing. The thought made her feel more guilty than ever that she should once more take advantage of their trust. But tonight, this one last time, she had to. There was no other way. She opened the door and slipped out into the heavy August night.

Leaving the cottage was like leaving something real and moving into dream. Her body felt weightless, and she seemed to float down the path to the gate. Jesse was there, waiting. Neither of them spoke. He took her hand and they ran together, lightly, down the road, past other sleeping cottages, into the dim and empty center of the village. The big glass windows here were lidded eyes that didn't care—that barely saw them, barely gave them back reflections. The blacksmith's shop, the mill, the church, the stores, so busy and alive in daylight, were hunched, deserted now, dark piles and shapes without a purpose or a meaning. And then, ahead, Winnie saw the jailhouse, its new wood still unpainted, lamplight spilling through a window at the front. And there, in the cleared yard behind it, like a great L upside down, was the gallows.

The sky flashed white. But this time it wasn't heat lightning, for a few moments later a low mumble, still far away, announced at last the coming storm. A fresh breeze lifted Winnie's hair, and from somewhere in the village behind them a dog barked.

Two shadows detached themselves from the gloom as Winnie and Jesse came up. Tuck pulled her to him and hugged her hard, and Miles squeezed her hand. No one said a word. Then the four of them crept to the back of the building. Here, too high for Winnie to see into, was a barred window through which, from the room in front, light glowed faintly. Winnie peered up at it, at the blackness of the bars with the dim gold of the light between. Into her head came lines from an old poem:

Stone walls do not a prison make,
Nor iron bars a cage.

Over and over the lines repeated themselves in her head till they were altogether meaningless. Another roll of thunder sounded. The storm was moving nearer.

Then Miles was standing on a box. He was pouring oil around the frame of the window. A swirl of wind brought the thick, rich smell of it down to Winnie's nostrils. Tuck handed up a tool and Miles began to pry at the nails securing the window frame. Miles knew carpentering. Miles could do the job. Winnie shivered and held tight to Jesse's hand. One nail was free. Another. Tuck reached up to receive them as they came out one by one. A fourth nail screeched as it was pried up, and Miles poured on more oil.

From the front of the jailhouse, the constable yawned noisily and began to whistle. The whistling came nearer. Miles dropped down. They heard the constable's footsteps coming up to Mae's cell. The barred door clanked. Then the footsteps receded, the whistling grew fainter. An inner door shut, and the lamp glow disappeared.

At once Miles was up again and prying at the nails. An eighth was out, a ninth, a tenth. Winnie counted carefully, while behind her counting, her mind sang, "Stone walls do not a prison make."

Miles handed down the prying tool. He grasped the bars of the window firmly, ready to pull, and stood poised. "What is he waiting for?" thought Winnie. "Why doesn't he . . ." Then—a flash of lightning and, soon after, a crack of thunder. In the midst of the noise, Miles gave a mighty heave. But the window did not budge.

The thunder ebbed. Winnie's heart sank. What if it was all impossible? What if the window would never come out? What if . . . She looked over her shoulder at the dark shape of the gallows, and shuddered.

Again a flash of lightning, and this time a crashing burst of noise from the swirling sky. Miles yanked. The window frame sprang free, and still grasping it by the bars, he tumbled backward off the box. The job was done.

Two arms appeared in the hole left by the missing frame. Mae! Her head appeared. It was too dark to see her face. The window—what if it was too small for her to squeeze through? What if . . . But now her shoulders were out. She groaned softly. Another flash of lightning lit her face for an instant and Winnie saw an expression there of deep concentration, tip of tongue protruding, brows furrowed.

Now Tuck was on the box, helping her, giving her his own shoulders to pull on, Miles and Jesse close at his sides, arms upstretched, eager to receive her bulk. Her hips were free—now, look out!—here she came, her skirts tearing on the rough edges of the boards, arms flailing—and they were all in a heap on the ground. Another crash of thunder muffled Jesse's bursting, exultant laugh. Mae was free.

Winnie clasped her trembling hands thankfully. And then the first drop of rain plopped precisely on the tip of her nose. The Tucks untangled themselves and turned to her. One by one, as the rain began, they drew her to them and kissed her. One by one she kissed them back. Was it rain on Mae's face? On Tuck's? Or was it tears? Jesse was last. He put his arms around her and hugged her tight, and whispered the single word, "Remember!"

Then Miles was on the box again, lifting her. Her hands grasped the edges of the window. This time she waited with him. When the thunder came, it tore the sky apart with its roar, and as it came, she pulled herself through, and dropped to the cot inside, unharmed. She looked up at the open square and saw the frame with Miles's hands holding it. The next obliging roll of thunder saw it wedged once more into place. And then—would Miles put back the nails? She waited.

Rain came in sheets now, riding the wind, flung crosswise through the night. Lightning crackled, a brilliant, jagged streak, and thunder rattled the little building. The tension in the parched earth eased and vanished. Winnie felt it go. The muscles of her stomach loosened, and all at once she was exhausted.

Still she waited. Would Miles put back the nails? At last, standing tiptoe on the cot, she grasped the bars of the window, pulling herself up till she could just see through. Rain blew into her face, but at the next flash of lightning, looking down, she saw that the yard was empty. And before the thunder followed, in a pause while wind and rain held back for one brief moment, she thought she heard, fading in the distance, the tinkling little melody of the music box. The Tucks—her darling Tucks—were gone.

25

The first week of August was long over. And now, though autumn was still some weeks away, there was a feeling that the year had begun its downward arc, that the wheel was turning again, slowly now, but soon to go faster, turning once more in its changeless sweep of change. Winnie, standing at the fence in front of the touch-me-not cottage, could hear the new note in the voices of the birds. Whole clouds of them lifted, chattering, into the sky above the wood, and then settled, only to lift again. Across the road, gold-enrod was coming into bloom. And an early-drying milkweed had opened its rough pod, exposing a host of downy-headed seeds. As she watched, one of these detached itself into a sudden breeze and sailed sedately off, while others leaned from the pod as if to observe its departure.

Winnie dropped down cross-legged on the grass. Two weeks had gone by since the night of the storm, the night of Mae Tuck's escape. And Mae had not been found. There was no trace of her at all, or of Tuck or Miles or Jesse. Winnie was profoundly grateful for that. But she was also profoundly tired. It had been a trying two weeks.

For the hundredth time she reviewed it all: how the constable had come into the cell soon after she had settled herself on the cot; how he had let down a shutter over the window to keep out the rain; how, then, he had stood over her as she hunched under the blanket, her breath heavy, trying to look as large as possible; how, finally, he had gone away and not come back till morning.

But she had not dared to sleep, for fear she would kick off the blanket and give herself away—give the Tucks away—unwittingly. So she had lain there, pulse thudding, eyes wide open. She would never forget the rattle of the rain on the jailhouse roof, or the smell of wet wood, or the darkness that had saved them all; or how difficult it was not to cough. She had wanted to cough as soon as it occurred to her that she mustn't, and she passed a long hour trying to swallow away the tickle that perversely constricted her throat. And she would never forget the crash outside that made her heart race, that she could not investigate, and did not understand till morning, when on the way home she saw that the gallows had blown over in the wind.

But oh!—it made her tremble still to remember the constable's face when he found her. She had heard first a bustling in the front of the jail, and smelled fresh coffee, and had sat up, stiff with apprehension. Then the inner door opened—the door, she now saw, which separated the office from the pair of cells—and in the light that streamed before him, the constable appeared, carrying a breakfast tray. He was whistling cheerfully. He came up to the barred door of her cell and looked in. And his whistling died on his lips as if it had run down and needed to be wound up again. But this comical astonishment lasted for a moment only. And then his face flushed red with anger.

Winnie had sat on the cot, eyes downcast, feeling very small—and very like a criminal. In fact, he was soon shouting that if she were older, he'd have to keep her there—that it *was* a crime, what she had done. She was . . . an accomplice. She had helped a murderer escape. She was, in fact, a criminal. But too young to be punished by the law. Worse luck, he told her, for she badly needed punishing.

She was released, then, into the custody of her mother and father. And these new words, "accomplice" and "custody," chilled her blood. Over and over they asked her, shocked at first and then wistful:

why had she *done* such a thing? *Why?* She was their daughter. They had trusted her. They had tried to bring her up properly, with a true sense of right and wrong. They did not understand. And finally she had sobbed the only truth there was into her mother's shoulder, the only explanation: the Tucks were her friends. She had done it because—in spite of everything, she loved them.

This of all things her family understood, and afterward they drew together staunchly around her. It was hard for them in the village, Winnie knew it was, and the knowledge gave her pain. For they were proud. And she had shamed them. Still, this side of the affair was not without its benefits, at least for Winnie. Though she was confined to the yard indefinitely and could go nowhere, not even with her mother or her grandmother, the other children wandered by to look at her, to talk to her through the fence. They were impressed by what she had done. She was a figure of romance to them now, where before she had been too neat, too prissy; almost, somehow, too *clean* to be a real friend.

Winnie sighed and plucked at the grass around her ankles. School would open soon. It wouldn't be so bad. In fact, she thought as her spirits lifted, this year it might be rather nice.

And then two things happened. First of all, the toad appeared out of the weeds, on her side of the road this time. It bounced out of a cover of old dandelion leaves and landed—plop!—just beyond the fence. If she had reached her hand through the bars, she could have touched it. And next, a large brown dog, with easy gait and dangling tongue, came loping down the road toward them. He stopped opposite the fence and looked at Winnie with a friendly swish of his tail, and then he saw the toad. At once he began to bark, his eyes bright. He pranced up, his hind quarters leaping independently from side to side, nose close to the toad, his voice shrill with enthusiasm.

"Don't!" cried Winnie, leaping to her feet and flapping her arms. "Go away, dog! Stop that! Go away—shoo!"

The dog paused. He looked up at Winnie's frantic dancing and then he looked at the toad, who had pressed down close to the dirt, eyes tight shut. It was too much for him. He began to bark again, and reached out a long paw.

"Oh!" cried Winnie. "Oh—*don't* do that! Leave my toad *alone!*" And before she had time to realize what she was doing, she bent, reached through the bars, and snatched the toad up and away from harm, dropping it on the grass inside the fence.

A feeling of revulsion swept through her. While the dog whined, pawing uselessly at the fence, she stood rigid, staring at the toad, wiping her hand again and again on the skirt of her dress. Then she remembered the actual feel of the toad, and the revulsion passed. She knelt and touched the skin of its back. It was rough and soft, both at once. And cool.

Winnie stood up and looked at the dog. He was waiting outside the fence, his head on one side, peering at her longingly. "It's *my* toad," Winnie told him. "So you'd better leave it alone." And then, on an impulse, she turned and ran into the cottage, up to her room, to the bureau drawer where she had hidden Jesse's bottle—the bottle of water from the spring. In a moment she was back again. The toad still squatted where she had dropped it, the dog still waited at the fence. Winnie pulled out the cork from the mouth of the bottle, and kneeling, she poured the precious water, very slowly and carefully, over the toad.

The dog watched this operation, and then, yawning, he was suddenly bored. He turned and loped away, back down the road to the village. Winnie picked up the toad and held it for a long time, without the least disgust, in the palm of her hand. It sat calmly, blinking, and the water glistened on its back.

The little bottle was empty now. It lay on the grass at Winnie's feet. But if all of it was true, there was more water in the wood. There was plenty more. Just in case. When she was seventeen. If she should decide, there was more water in the wood. Winnie smiled. Then she stooped and put her hand through the fence and set the toad free. "There!" she said. "You're safe. Forever."

Epilogue

The sign said WELCOME TO TREEGAP, but it was hard to believe that this was really Treegap. The main street hadn't changed so very much, but there were many other streets now, crossing the main street. The road itself was blacktopped. There was a white line painted down its center.

Mae and Tuck, on the seat of a clattering wooden wagon, bumped slowly into Treegap behind the fat old horse. They had seen continuous change and were accustomed to it, but here it seemed shocking and sad. "Look," said Tuck. "Look, Mae. Ain't that where the wood used to be? It's gone! Not a stick or a stump left! And her cottage—that's gone, too."

It was very hard to recognize anything, but from the little hill, which had once lain outside the village and was now very much a part of it, they thought they could figure things out. "Yes," said Mae, "that's where it was, I do believe. 'Course, it's been so long since we was here, I can't tell for certain."

There was a gas station there now. A young man in greasy coveralls was polishing the windshield of a wide and rusty Hudson automobile. As Mae and Tuck rolled past, the young man grinned and said to the driver of the Hudson, who lounged at the wheel, "Looky there. In from the country for a big time." And they chuckled together.

Mae and Tuck clattered on into the village proper, past a catholic mixture of houses which soon gave way to shops and other places of business: a hot-dog stand; a dry cleaner; a pharmacy; a five-and-ten; another gas station; a tall, white frame building with a pleasant verandah, The Treegap Hotel—Family Dining, Easy Rates. The post office. Beyond that, the jailhouse, but a larger jailhouse now, painted brown, with an office for the county clerk. A black and white police car was parked in front, with a red glass search-light on its roof and a radio antenna, like a buggy whip, fastened to the windshield.

Mae glanced at the jailhouse, but looked away quickly. "See beyond there?" she said, pointing. "That diner? Let's stop there and get a cup of coffee. All right?"

"All right," said Tuck. "Maybe they'll know something."

Inside, the diner gleamed with chrome and smelled like linoleum and ketchup. Mae and Tuck took seats on rumbling swivel stools at the long counter. The counterman emerged from the kitchen at the rear and sized them up expertly. They looked all right. A little queer, maybe—their clothes, especially—but honest. He slapped a cardboard menu down in front of them and leaned on the foaming orangeade cooler. "You folks from off?" he asked.

"Yep," said Tuck. "Just passing through."

"Sure," said the counterman.

"Say," said Tuck cautiously, fingering the menu. "Didn't there used to be a wood once, down the other side of town?"

"Sure," said the counterman. "Had a big electrical storm, though, about three years ago now or thereabouts. Big tree got hit by lightning, split right down the middle. Caught fire and everything. Tore up the ground, too. Had to bulldoze her all out."

"Oh," said Tuck. He and Mae exchanged glances.

"Coffee, please," said Mae. "Black. For both of us."

"Sure," said the counterman. He took the menu away, poured coffee into thick pottery mugs, and leaned again on the orangeade cooler.

"Used to be a fresh-water spring in that wood," said Tuck boldly, sipping his coffee.

"Don't know nothing about that," said the counterman. "Had to bulldoze her all out, like I say."

"Oh," said Tuck.

Afterward, while Mae was shopping for supplies, Tuck went back through the town on foot—back the way they had come—out to the little hill. There were houses there now, and a feed-and-grain store, but on the far side of the hill, inside a rambling iron fence, was a cemetery.

Tuck's heart quickened. He had noticed the cemetery on the way in. Mae had seen it, too. They had not spoken about it. But both knew it might hold other answers. Tuck straightened his old jacket. He passed through an archway of wrought-iron curlicues, and paused, squinting at the weedy rows of gravestones. And then, far over to the right, he saw a tall monument, once no doubt imposing but now tipped slightly sidewise. On it was carved one name: Foster.

Slowly, Tuck turned his footsteps toward the monument. And saw, as he approached, that there were other, smaller markers all around it. A family plot. And then his throat closed. For it was there. He had wanted it to be there, but now that he saw it, he was overcome with sadness. He knelt and read the inscription:

"So," said Tuck to himself. "Two years. She's been gone two years." He stood up and looked around, embarrassed, trying to clear the lump from his throat. But there was no one to see him. The cemetery was very quiet. In the branches of a willow behind him, a red-winged blackbird chirped. Tuck wiped his eyes hastily. Then he straightened his jacket again and drew up his hand in a brief salute. "Good girl," he said aloud. And then he turned and left the cemetery, walking quickly.

Later, as he and Mae rolled out of Treegap, Mae said softly, without looking at him, "She's gone?"

Tuck nodded. "She's gone," he answered.

There was a long moment of silence between them, and then Mae said, "Poor Jesse."

"He knowed it, though," said Tuck. "At least, he knowed she wasn't coming. We all knowed that, long time ago."

"Just the same," said Mae. She sighed. And then she sat up a little straighter. "Well, where to now, Tuck? No need to come back here no more."

"That's so," said Tuck. "Let's just head on out this way. We'll locate something."

"All right," said Mae. And then she put a hand on his arm and pointed. "Look out for that toad."

Tuck had seen it, too. He reined in the horse and climbed down from the wagon. The toad was squatting in the middle of the road, quite unconcerned. In the other lane, a pickup truck rattled by, and against the breeze it made, the toad shut its eyes tightly. But it did not move. Tuck waited till the truck had passed, and then he picked up the toad and carried it to the weeds along the road's edge. "Durn fool thing must think it's going to live forever," he said to Mae.

And soon they were rolling on again, leaving Treegap behind, and as they went, the tinkling little melody of a music box drifted out behind them and was lost at last far down the road.

Literature Circle Questions

Use these questions and activities that follow to get more out of the experience of reading Tuck Everlasting by Natalie Babbitt.

1. In the prologue, the author describes three things that happen on one day and then come together in a strange way. What are those three things?

2. What does Winnie see in the woods that causes the Tucks to kidnap her?

3. What happened to the Tucks that made them realize that the spring water they drank was magical?

4. Compare the Tucks with Winnie's family. What does Winnie like better about the Tuck family?

5. Explain why the man in the yellow suit follows Winnie to the Tuck's house. What does he hope to gain?

6. What advice would you give Winnie about being with the Tucks? Would you tell her to stay or run away?

7. Why does Tuck take Winnie out in the rowboat? What message does he give her about living forever?

8. What motive does Mae Tuck have for killing the man in the yellow suit? What arguments do you have to support her action? What arguments do you have against it?

Note: The literature circle questions are keyed to Bloom's Taxonomy: Knowledge: 1-3; Comprehension: 4-5; Application: 6-7; Analysis: 8-9; Synthesis: 10-11; Evaluation: 12-14.

9. Why is Winnie so worried about Mae Tuck going to the gallows? What things might happen if she did?

10. How would the story be different if the man in the yellow suit had not died? What might have happened to the world and the Tucks?

11. What meaning does the toad have for Winnie? Why do you think she pours the magical water over it? What do we learn about the toad in the epilogue to the story?

12. If you had the same choice as Winnie, would you have taken a drink of the spring water? Why or why not?

13. Why do you think Natalie Babbitt wrote this book? What thoughts does she want to share with her readers?

14. Do you think that Winnie led a happy life? How do you think the Tucks may have changed the way she lived?

Activities

• Draw an illustrated map of the main settings in Tuck Everlasting. Label the places that play an important role in the story.

• Imagine that you could choose to stay the same age forever. What age would you choose? List three reasons why you would want to be that age. Then list three problems with staying that age forever.

• Imagine that the Tucks are everlasting and still wandering the earth. Write a description of them if they came into your town this year. Describe where you might see them, what they would be doing, and how you would recognize them.

OPEN MIC

OPEN MIC

Riffs on Life Between Cultures
in Ten Voices

edited by

Mitali Perkins

CANDLEWICK PRESS

Compilation and introduction copyright © 2013 by Mitali Perkins
"Becoming Henry Lee" copyright © 2013 by David Yoo
"Why I Won't Be Watching the *Last Airbender* Movie"
copyright © 2010 by Gene Luen Yang
"Talent Show" copyright © 2013 by Cherry Cheva
"Voilà!" copyright © 2013 by Debbie Rigaud
"Three-Pointer" copyright © 2013 by Mitali Perkins
"Like Me" copyright © 2013 by Varian Johnson
"Confessions of a Black Geek"
copyright © 2013 by Olugbemisola Rhuday-Perkovich
"Under Berlin" copyright © 2013 by G. Neri
"Brotherly Love" copyright © 2013 by Francisco X. Stork
"Lexicon" copyright © 2013 by Naomi Shihab Nye

The traditional verse on page 114 is from *Poems for the Children's Hour*, compiled by Josephine Bouton (New York: Platt & Munk, 1945).

First edition 2013

Library of Congress Catalog Card Number 2012955218
ISBN 978-0-7636-5866-3

13 14 15 16 17 18 BVG 10 9 8 7 6 5 4 3 2 1

Printed in Berryville, VA, U.S.A.

This book was typeset in Stone Print and Stone Sans.

Candlewick Press
99 Dover Street
Somerville, Massachusetts 02144

visit us at www.candlewick.com

To my nephews, Jason and Jordan,
who know about life between cultures

CONTENTS

Introduction

Conversations about race can be so *serious*, right? People get all tense or touchy. The best way to ease the situation is with humor. There's actually a lot of bizarre comedy material when it comes to growing up "between cultures," as I like to call it. It's a weird place.

Take being Indian-American, for example. Why did that lady at the grocery store feel compelled to tell me about her random bad experience with chicken tikka masala? Do I want to know? We don't even eat chicken tikka masala in my part of India. It's just as orange and soupy and strange to me as it is to her.

And did that dude *really* just ask if I know his doctor? There are over a billion of us on the planet—why should

Dr. So-and-So-ji and I be best buddies? (It's even stranger when I *do* know his Indian doctor, which happened once.)

Then there's the boring dinner party conversation during which an artsy type describes — in lengthy detail, ad nauseum — the plot of that one Bollywood movie he simply *adored.* I grew up with those "fillums," man. There are a bunch of them. It only makes things worse when you apply a weird lilting accent, add a head waggle, and laugh hilariously at yourself. Awkward.

What works better (at least for me) is when *I* share stories about how strange it was to be squeezed between cultures. Like when I was seven and wondered why the fat guy in the red suit skipped our house completely in December. And then some stupid bunny forgot to come in April. Or later, in high school, wanting desperately to date guys, which wasn't going to happen because (a) I was the color of pastrami and they preferred provolone, and (b) my parents dated *after* they met and got married, both of which happened on the same day.

When I tell my stories, I want listeners to laugh (not *at* me, I hope, but *with* me). Humor has the power to break down barriers and draw us together across borders. Once you've shared a laugh with someone, it's almost impossible to see them as "other." Poking fun at my marginalized life also sets readers free to see the funny in their own lives, a key to surviving the stressful experience of becoming an adult.

I do have some ground rules, however, for what I consider good humor, especially in a tension-filled arena like race. Here they are, take them or leave them:

1. Good humor pokes fun at the powerful—not the weak. Using the gift of wit to pummel someone less gifted physically, socially, emotionally, or intellectually may win a few initial laughs. Soon, though, audiences sense the power-flexing of a bully behind the humor, and they'll stop listening. The most powerful person of all, of course, is the storyteller (see rule #3), so no holds barred when it comes to humbling that target.

2. Good humor builds affection for the "other." At the close of a story, poem, or joke about race or ethnicity, do we feel closer to people who are the subject of the humor? If not, even if the piece is hilarious, it's not *good* funny. Sometimes comedians use wit to alienate the "other" from us instead of drawing us closer to one another. Again, they may get a few laughs, but they're cheap laughs. Of course, I don't like *any* humor where someone gets hurt—I rooted for Wile E. Coyote, winced at the Marx brothers' physical (painful) humor, and stand stony-faced while my sons laugh at videos of people falling and crashing into things. So take rule #2 with a caveat: if watching someone take a hit or a blow makes you like them better, you might appreciate some humor that I don't. And that's okay.

3. Good humor is usually self-deprecatory (note: not self-defecatory, although it can feel like that). While I usually don't like edicts about who can write about whom, in a post-9/11 North America, where segregation, slavery, and even genocide aren't too far back in history, funny multicultural stories work best when the author shares the protagonist's race or culture. Funny is powerful, and that's why in this case it does matter who tells a story. Writing that explores issues of race and ethnicity with a touch of humor must stay closer to memoir than other kinds of fiction on the spectrum of storytelling. Some writers and comedians have succeeded in poking fun across borders, but it's challenging in today's mine-filled conversations about race. Go ahead if you want to try, I tell them, but don't say I didn't warn you.

Okay, enough with the rules. Time for some lighthearted story-telling about the between-cultures life. I'm thrilled about the authors who have contributed to this anthology. Some pieces, like Cherry Cheva's "Talent Show," Debbie Rigaud's *"Voilà!"* and David Yoo's "Becoming Henry Lee," make us chuckle; others, like Greg Neri's "Under Berlin," Francisco Stork's "Brotherly Love," my "Three-Pointer," and Varian Johnson's "Like Me," may bring a rueful, ouch-filled smile. Gene Luen Yang's "Why I Won't Be Watching the *Last Airbender* Movie," Olugbemisola Rhuday-Perkovich's "Confessions of a Black Geek," and Naomi Shihab Nye's "Lexicon" make us feel like we're exchanging a knowing glance of shared humor with the storyteller or poet—like viewers are supposed to feel when cast members on popular sitcoms catch the camera's eye for a moment.

When you're done reading, or if something strikes your fancy, find us on Facebook (facebook.com/openmicanthology) to let us know what you think, and share your own weird, funny, or crazy story about growing up between cultures.

Laughing with you, not at you,
Mitali Perkins

Becoming Henry Lee

DAVID YOO

Ching Chong's real name was Henry Choi Lee, but when he started the eighth grade, one of his classmates called him Ching Chong and it stuck. At first this bothered him — who wants to be called Ching Chong, after all? — but it would soon turn out that what his classmates called him was the least of his problems.

Before his father was transferred to Connecticut for his job, the Lees lived in southern California, where Henry was surrounded by other Asian students. But at Renham Middle School in Renham, Connecticut, he was the only Asian kid.

Renham was an affluent town and home to the best high school in Connecticut, which was the main reason Henry's parents had moved there. They wanted to give their son a leg up toward getting into an Ivy League university, which would then give him the best chance of eventually becoming a doctor or lawyer. "A doctor or lawyer command respect in community," they'd often say.

"So does proper grammar," Henry would retort, but they'd ignore him.

The adult Lees fit some of the Asian stereotypes nicely. But not Henry. Everyone at school assumed he was a nerd. They were certain he was a whiz at numbers, music, video games, and kung fu. Like all Asians must be.

But in fact, Henry was horrible at math and could hardly play the piano despite the private lessons his parents had arranged for him since he was four. He got dizzy playing first-person shooter games because of a balance problem caused by the perpetual inflammation of his inner ear. Which also meant that when it came to martial arts, Henry was clueless.

Within a month of starting eighth grade in this new town, Henry decided that he absolutely hated being Korean. Or rather, he didn't like being different. He made it his main goal to change people's perceptions of him. So he never studied and swore off video games (which he didn't like playing anyway) and Asian food.

At the Renham Galleria food court, Henry made it a point to eat pizza (even though the slices were always a little cold) and avoided the comic-book store and gaming depot. The cool white boys in his grade sat with their equally cool girl-friends, whose dyed hair always came out kind of blue-looking instead of the intended black, and ate the teriyaki combo #3 from Chang Gourmet after spending hours reading manga and trading used video games.

Another problem, at least as Henry saw it, was that people could tell from a mile away that he was Asian. So Henry started wearing white baseball caps with the brim pushed down low, trying to hide his jet-black hair and smaller, upper-eyelid-deprived Asian eyes. One weekend, after watching an episode of some Nickelodeon show where the star had bright blond hair and was beloved by everyone, he ran out to the store, bought a bottle of Color-Me-Blond, and dyed his hair. At school on Monday, he hated himself for not thinking through his decision. Kids kept asking him if "the carpet matched the drapes," which Henry didn't quite understand, given that they'd never before seemed interested enough to inquire about his house, though deep down he had a feeling it had something to do with the fact that his newly blond hair clashed with his still-black eyebrows.

Kids also teased Henry by pretending to talk in broken English, even though he had a perfectly good American accent. He decided he had to make it even more obvious that he didn't speak the way they thought a Korean would. The following weekend, he decided to adopt a southern accent, so he rummaged through his parents' old DVD collection. Unfortunately for Henry, the one movie the Lees owned that took place in the South was their boxed set of *Roots*, an epic

TV miniseries about slavery. That Monday students were more confused than convinced by his new accent.

"Late for class again, Ching Chong?" a kid asked as Henry struggled to open his lock.

"Never you mind, boy," Henry replied in his best *Roots* voice. "I hear tell the teacher's fixing to be late for class on account of the coffee machine in the lounge being done busted, so he gone have to get his coffee from down yonder in the cafeteria where done—"

"Chinese sure sounds a lot like English," the kid said. "What the heck did you just say?"

Dashing off to class, Henry tried to get a laugh by insulting the teacher in his new voice. "Lawd almighty, I done hear tell you smells right like a hawse," he told her. Sadly, his classmates didn't understand what the heck he was saying. The teacher must have, though, because she gave him three days of detention.

For the rest of the day, Henry simplified his southern accent by sticking the word *ain't* into every other sentence. Nobody paid much attention. Obviously, his linguistic efforts were failing to convince anyone that he was a white boy whose daddy owned a plantation.

When Henry's mom picked him up after school, Henry was so depressed that he didn't see her pull up. She rolled down the driver's side window and hollered, "Henry! You get in car, now!"

"Yeah, Ching Chong, you get in car, now!" the other kids hooted.

Henry hurried to the car, embarrassed by his mom's broken English. The next afternoon, even though he lived several miles away, Henry walked home after detention. His mom saw him walking down West Renham Road and slammed on the brakes.

"What are you doing? Traffic is dangerous! Get in car now!" she shouted.

"Thought I'd save you some gas," Henry said, looking around feverishly before diving into the backseat.

Thanks to the unchangeable shape of his eyes and his parents' undeniable Asian accents, Henry realized he was never going to convince his peers that he was white. It was going to take a miracle for things to turn around, but luckily for Henry, a miracle was waiting for him in study hall the first day back from winter break: Marcy Spetucchi, the most popular girl in the eighth grade. And although she had never said a word to Henry before, when Marcy saw Henry sitting there all alone, she asked him out of the blue, "You're good at math, Ching Chong. Can you help me with my homework?"

Up to this moment, Henry had always gotten frustrated when classmates asked him for help on math homework, but this time, he agreed. Marcy was too pretty to deny. As he taught her how to do math, making up rules and formulas as he went along, he realized that he'd finally stumbled upon the solution to his social woes. He'd been going about it all wrong, it turned out; rather than trying to convince everyone he wasn't Asian, the key was to become über-Asian. Wasn't this proof? For the first time ever, Henry Choi Lee was hanging out with the most popular girl in school.

After school that day, he accompanied his one sort-of friend (a pale, perpetually bloody-nosed kid named Sam, who lived down the street) to the mall, where they happened upon a group of kids from a rival middle school talking smack with kids from Renham.

Henry decided to test his new theory. He stalked over to the fight, crouched low, and started growling and shoving air around with his hands.

At first his classmates looked as stunned by his maneuver as their rivals, but then one of them moved closer to Henry. "You mess with us, you mess with the Karate Kid," he said.

"Yeah, Henry could kick anyone's butt at Farnham," another one added. "He's got a fourth-degree black belt in kung fu."

"For real?" one of the Farnham middle-schoolers asked.

Henry nodded and kept yowling. For the first time, he saw his classmates beam at him.

"Why's your nose bleeding?" the rival kid asked Sam.

"He got out of line," Henry muttered ominously.

The Farnham kids backed off, and his classmates gleefully patted him on the back. As Henry fist-bumped them one by one, he wondered why he'd hated stereotypes so much. What was so wrong with people mistakenly assuming he was a genius? That he was good at math and science? That he was a martial arts master? Obviously the key was to prove that he was the most *Asian* Asian student in the history of middle school.

That weekend he did research online on how to be Asian and began crafting a persona that incorporated all the major elements of Asian-ness imaginable. His first move was to use tai chi and meditation.

In gym class, Mark Porter shouted in pain as his back seized up from trying to do a pull-up. As he writhed around like a grub on the cushioned mat while the rest of the class and the gym teacher stared at him in fascination, Henry gravely walked to Mark and stood over him. He clapped his hands loudly once to get everyone's attention, then proceeded to rub them really fast like he was trying to warm them up. Mark looked up at Henry, puzzled but still making appropriate sounds of pain.

"I will now use tai chi to help your back feel better," Henry said, and closing his eyes, he proceeded to move his arms in a dance-like motion à la Mr. Miyagi, pretending to shoot waves of *chi* into Mark's back.

A moment later, Mark stopped groaning. "I think I feel something," he said, keeping his eyes on Henry.

"Usually you do tai chi on yourself, to relieve stress,"

Henry explained, "but if you're really one with the life force, it's okay to use it on others. What I'm doing here is redirecting positive energy to your back while at the same time pulling away the . . . er . . . evil energy." Henry shook his head slightly as he concentrated with his eyes closed.

"It's working!" Mark said.

Henry opened his eyes. Everyone, even the gym teacher, was looking at him like he was some kind of Zen wizard.

By the next morning, circles were forming around Henry wherever he went. Students wanted to see him perform tai chi again, but they were hesitant. Finally, a kid asked if Henry could help his strained wrist feel better.

"I only have a certain amount of *chi* to work with each week. Maybe next week," Henry said.

"But—" the student protested.

"I said be ready for you next week!" Henry shouted, imitating the angry Chinese dry cleaner who yelled that exact same grammatically incorrect sentence at his dad any time Mr. Lee tried to pick up his dress shirts.

Some of the students didn't believe in Henry's magical tai chi abilities, so in homeroom, he decided to prove them wrong. Extending a stiff index finger, he zapped one of the beta fish in the bowl on Mr. Parson's desk with a dollop of invisible *chi*. Nothing happened.

"The fish is fine," a skeptic noted.

"Not so, young grasshopper," Henry said, lightly patting

the kid on the back. "I just used *chi* to scramble its internal organs. You'll see: in a few days that fish will be dead."

Sure enough, a few mornings later, the students arrived to find one of the beta fish lying sideways at the top of the water. Everyone was officially convinced that Henry was a tai chi master. No one seemed to remember that before Henry's zap, beta fish seemed to die every few days since they didn't have long life spans to begin with.

The kid with the wrist injury approached him again for his services.

"It seems pretty serious," Henry said, feeling the kid's wrist. "We might need to do some acupuncture. I don't have my needles with me. Why don't you go sharpen a half-dozen pencils, and we'll see what we can do about this wrist pain you speak of."

The kid raced off without a moment's hesitation, and Henry was taken aback. Wasn't the threat of getting punctured by pencils enough to deter this patient? The kid returned, clutching a handful of newly sharpened pencils. "Um, wait—are those lead pencils?" Henry stalled. "Yeah, no, that's not going to work. Let's just stick with the tai chi."

Pretending to know stuff was exhausting. Henry almost fell asleep in English class. The teacher shouted for him to wake up, and Henry, startled at first, glanced at his peers before explaining, "I wasn't sleeping. I was meditating."

The teacher rolled her eyes, and Henry leaned over to

James Murphy to whisper, "I used my meditation to visualize tomorrow's multiple-choice quiz. Choose *B* when you don't know the answer."

This, of course, hadn't come from meditating. The "*B* strategy" was something he'd learned about multiple-choice questions when his parents had forced him to take a PSAT training course the summer before.

The best part about amping up his Asian-ness was that he got to spend time with Marcy Spetucchi. Because he was bad at math, Marcy didn't learn how to do the problems correctly. When she failed her next quiz, Henry shrugged and said, "I guess you're going to have to work harder at it." She begged Henry to be her full-time math tutor every day after school. "You're not like the other boys," she said, smiling shyly at him.

Two more failed quizzes later, and Marcy finally realized the real reason he was different from the other boys: he was really, really bad at math, and something of a compulsive liar. She promptly fired him. Or dumped him. Depending on whom you asked. However, others had noticed them spending time together, and by the end of the year, people seemed to see Henry in a new light. In fact, nobody called him Ching Chong anymore!

Summer came and went with more SAT prep. When Henry got to Renham High, he was ready to take his role of Super Asian Man to the next level. Unfortunately, he ran into a problem. There was one other Asian student in the high school, Timmy Nguyen, valedictorian of the senior class, which changed everything. The whole student body now regularly mistook Henry (mistakenly or intentionally—what difference did it make?) for this Nguyen fellow, even though the senior was Vietnamese and looked nothing like Henry (the guy even had a full mustache and Henry hadn't started shaving). Upper-class nerds shoved Henry into the lockers, assuming that (a) he was Timmy, or (b) he was a curve buster just like Timmy, even though Henry was bombing his classes and hurtling toward a decidedly un-Asian low GPA. His own former classmates from middle school ignored him again, since being unquestionably Asian was not considered cool at Renham High.

One weekend Henry's parents rented the movie *The Departed*, in which two white actors—Leonardo DiCaprio and Matt Damon—played foes. As they watched the crime drama together, Henry was stunned to discover that his parents had mistaken the two actors for the same person. They were convinced the movie was a psychological thriller about one white guy who had multiple personalities warring with each other in his head.

"Hold on," his dad said, pointing at the screen for the dozenth time. "Is he the good cop now or the bad cop?"

Suddenly Henry was beyond mad—his white classmates thought all Asian guys looked the same, and his parents thought all white guys looked the same, too? Was he the only person on the planet who noticed that people of the same race weren't all twins or clones? "You guys are racist!" Henry shouted, and ran upstairs to his room.

His father eventually followed him upstairs and sat next to Henry on the edge of his bed. It was equally uncomfortable for them both. When his father asked what was wrong, Henry explained everything: from when he'd first started school in Renham to now, when everyone was mistaking him for Timmy Nguyen.

Mr. Lee thought about this for a minute before responding. "Well, things could be worse," he said. "For instance, take this Timmy Nguyen person. Imagine the poor guy, being mistaken for *you*."

This failed to cheer Henry up, so his father thought about it some more.

"Maybe if you give classmates something to identify you, they don't think you're someone else," he said. "Besides, you need do more extracurricular activities so you stand out to admissions committees at Ivies."

Clearly his father was still trying to get Henry to become the cliché Asian son he'd always wanted, but Henry decided to take his advice anyway. The next morning, when his homeroom teacher asked for a volunteer to help a classmate read a scene for drama-club auditions, Henry raised his hand. After hearing Henry's line reading, the classmate encouraged him to try out for the play.

At the audition, everyone was stunned at how good an actor Henry was.

"Do you have any experience?" the drama teacher asked.

"Not really," Henry said, but he realized this wasn't entirely true, because ever since moving to Renham, he'd been acting—wasn't the definition of acting pretending to be somebody you weren't?

"You're a natural," the drama teacher said.

And so just like that, Henry finally found himself a full-fledged member of a group. After tryouts, they headed for the late buses, where they ran into the JV wrestling team, who shouted, "Drama queens!" and "Fairy losers!"

The actors were furious and shot back insults, but not Henry. He smiled blissfully, repeating the taunts in his head as if they were the most beautiful sounds he'd ever heard.

Drama queens . . . Fairy losers . . .

The plural was music to his ears.

WHY I WON'T BE WATCHING THE LAST AIRBENDER MOVIE

GENE LUEN YANG

Derek was the first to tell me about it.

I knew they would do something like this! *I knew it!*

Award-winning cartoonist Derek Kirk Kim

It's an Asian fetishist's *dream!* All the Asian culture you could want without any of those pesky Asian people!

We've gotta respond in some way!

And so we did.

Derek wrote a blog post explaining our anger and advocating for a boycott.

LOWBRIGHT.COM

Tuesday, January 20, 2009

New day in politics, same old racist world on the silver screen

This past Monday, on Martin Luther King Jr.'s birthday, on the eve of Barack Obama's inauguration, I discovered that the casting of the four leading characters for the upcoming live-action movie, "The Last Airbender" (based on the TV show, "Avatar: The Last Airbender"), had gone entirely to white actors. I want—no, need—to say something about this.

I drew a webcomic doing the same. I posted it on my website a month before the movie's release.

WHY I WON'T BE WATCHING THE LAST AIRBENDER MOVIE

A friend turned me on to the original *Avatar: The Last Airbender* animated series on Nickelodeon, and from the first episode, I was hooked!

Gene Luen Yang, author of *American Born Chinese*

Here was an American cartoon with multi-faceted characters and addictive plot lines, all set in a beautifully constructed Asian fantasy world.

The writing was not only witty, thoughtful, and clever; it also showed a deep respect for and knowledge of Asian cultures. Even my wife loved it, and she usually avoids cartoons like the plague.

Don't you see?! The politics of the Fire Nation reflect those of Japan during the Meiji Restoration!

Shut up. They're gonna fight again.

When I heard that they were going to make a live-action adaptation, I was *thrilled*--

Oh, my flying Appas! That's gonna be amazing!

--until I learned they'd given the roles of the major heroic characters--all of whom were Asian or Inuit in the cartoon--to white actors.

What?!

Look, don't you want to live in a color-blind society? Maybe the most qualified actors for those roles just happened to be white!

Maybe...

Airbender's advocate

...but then how do you explain the original casting calls, which clearly indicated a preference for white actors from the get-go?

12-15 years old, Male, **Caucasian or any other ethnicity.** We are looking for a young man to play the lead role in a motion picture franchise. He must be athletic and

...

I got nothin'.

The casting decisions behind *The Last Airbender* movie make a clear, and clearly repugnant, statement:

Asian-American faces are simply inadequate for American audiences, even in a movie that so obviously celebrates our cultural heritage.

Look, I know how tiring it is to keep track of all the causes the modern world throws at us.

Paper or plastic?

Neither! I brought my own canvas bags!

But those are made by child labor!

And in the grand scheme of things, racism in the casting of a Hollywood popcorn flick, no matter how blatant, really isn't all that important. That's why I'm not asking you to picket or write letters or wear a T-shirt with a catchy slogan.

But if you want a T-shirt with a catchy slogan, Racebending.com has 'em!

AANG CAN STAY ASIAN AND STILL SAVE THE WORLD

ASIAN AND STILL SAVE

I'm just asking you, especially on July 2, 2010, and the weekend after, to spend your entertainment dollars on something other than *The Last Airbender* movie.

Thanks for taking the time to hear me out!

Of all the things I've ever posted on the Internet, my *Airbender* boycott comic drew the most attention.

Look at all these comments!

Most of the comments were well reasoned and respectful, even when the writer didn't agree with me.

@!#?@!

Yikes!

Most.

One of the folks who read my webcomic was an editor at Dark Horse Comics. She got in touch.

So you're a fan of the *Airbender* cartoon, huh?

Yep. But not the movie.

Me neither.

Would you be interested in writing Dark Horse's upcoming *Avatar: The Last Airbender* graphic novel series?

Will the graphic novels have anything to do with the movie?

Nope. They'll continue the story from the original cartoon. They won't reference the movie at--

YES-I-WANT-THAT-JOB-RIGHT-NOW!!!

Moral of the story? If something bugs you about the world, say something. Do it respectfully and give good reasons.

Who knows what might happen?

TALENT SHOW

CHERRY CHEVA

Question: There are two high-school juniors in a room. They're waiting to audition for the talent show. One is an Asian girl. The other is a white guy. One is tuning a violin. The other fiddles with a scrap of paper containing notes for a stand-up comedy act.

Which one is which?

Yeah. I know what you'd say. That's what I'd say, too, except that I happened to be the guy. Holding the violin. On which I was about to play Fritz Kreisler's "Praeludium and Allegro." Hopefully in a non-sucky way.

And then there was the girl with the scrap of paper. She was tiny and cute and already sitting there when I walked in — we were the last two auditions of the day — and I knew who she was, though we'd never spoken. The last time I'd seen her was two years ago in personal fitness class, which is what they call gym at our school. It was usually taught by Mr. Choffley, a very, very in-shape gay guy who liked nothing better than calling his students fatties and mocking the contents of their lunch bags. But the semester I took it, Mr. Choffley was on sabbatical,[1] so we had Ms. Hain. She was normally just the chemistry teacher, and while she cared very much if you were wearing goggles while wielding a pipette of sulfuric acid in lab, she didn't give a crap what you did in personal fitness, as long as you were physically moving the whole time.

And so I spent a semester's worth of Tuesday and Thursday afternoons walking during fifth period. As did the girl who now sat before me. We'd both stroll lazily around the track, and since her pace was slower (*impressively* slower, actually) than mine, every once in a while I'd lap her. And nod as I did so. And get a nod back. We never had a class together again, but now here she was. Still tiny. Still cute. And there was nobody else in the room, and her audition wasn't for another eight minutes, and I was nervous as hell about my own audition, and when I'm nervous, I like to distract myself.[2]

Here went nothing.

"Hey," I said as I sat down. "Gretchen, right?"

She looked up at me, startled, and then I saw it slowly

---

1. We later found out it was a yoga retreat in the Bahamas called, for some reason, Agony & Ecstasy. It may not have been a yoga retreat.

register on her face. The register turned into realization, which turned into a smile. "Personal fitness," she said.

I nodded.

"Josh?"

Oh. She knew my name, too. I hadn't expected it. "Yeah. I don't think we ever introduced ourselves, but . . ."

"Yeah, I don't know, I just heard along the way or something. . . ."

"Yeah, same here."

"Yeah."

Silence.

"So what's your talent?" I asked. I couldn't discern it from looking at her.

"Well," she answered, pulling a scrap of paper out of her pocket and waving it in my general direction; I could see messily scrawled notes in purple ink. "I don't know if I have a talent for it yet. But hopefully it's, um . . . stand-up comedy."

The words were out of my mouth before I could stop them: "That's not very Asian."

She seemed amused instead of offended, thank God,

2. Because the alternative, which was what happened last year, is for my hands to get so sweaty that my bow slips right out of my fingers and breaks. My old bow cost six hundred dollars, so you can imagine how happy my parents were. My new one cost seventy-five on craigslist, and I had to drive all the way across town to pick it up, at some dude's garage that appeared to be housing a ferret-breeding facility, so you can imagine how happy I was.

raising an eyebrow as she glanced down at my violin. "Your talent isn't particularly Jewish."

Hey, look at that. She knew more about me than just my name and the fact that we'd had gym together. That was promising. "It's not *non*-Jewish," I pointed out. "Plenty of famous Jewish violinists."

"True," she agreed. "A non-Jewish talent would be, like, flashing some foreskin and then performing feats of strength."

I burst out laughing. "I hope that's one of your jokes."

"It isn't."

"Okay, well, tell me a joke, then. Do part of your act."

"No." She seemed almost horrified that I'd asked.

"Come on!"

"Hell no!" She crumpled up her notes and stuffed them back in her pocket.

"If you're too scared to tell one person, how are you gonna tell a whole audience?" Oops. Gretchen was now scowling. I had clearly crossed the line from "Hey, he's interested in my act, how flattering" to "Who is this belligerent dipwad, and would an uppercut or a right cross be the best way to punch him in the face?"

"That's completely the wrong logic," she snapped. "People laugh more when there's more people."

As if on cue, we suddenly heard muffled laughter through the audition-room door. "Who's in there?" I asked.

"Ballet dancer."

"Yikes." I pictured some girl twirling around and then falling on her head or something—although that probably wouldn't make the teachers running the auditions laugh. Kids, maybe. Me, certainly.[3] But not teachers.

"She probably just said something cute. Or did something cute. I heard them laugh when she first went in, too." Now we heard a smattering of applause, and Gretchen pulled out her paper again and started fiddling with it. "Okay, now I'm getting nervous."

"I've *been* nervous," I said. "Welcome to my hell."

"I'm pretty sure I'm gonna screw it up."

"Oh, you are not."

"No, I probably am." She said this very matter-of-factly, as if her voice wasn't concerned, but her hands sure looked like they were. They weren't shaking, they just looked . . . tense.

"So?" I asked. "What's the worst that could happen? Last year I was so nervous I dropped my bow and it broke." I'm third chair in the school orchestra, so it's not like I can't play in front of an audience, but the competitive aspect of auditioning makes normal performance butterflies into an entirely

3. Assuming no grievous injuries occurred. I, despite what Katie Finkelstein would tell you about a certain second-grade field trip to a working dairy farm, am not a monster. I had nothing to do with that cow kicking her in the head, although I did laugh; again, this was only because it was clear that she wasn't injured. Just hilariously humiliated. (Fine, seven-year-old me was sort of a monster. I've mellowed with age.)

different, well, animal. Butterflies on steroids. Butterflies with Uzis and anger-management problems.

"Oh, I'm sorry!"

"It's fine, I got a new one." I held up my bow. "Seriously though, if you don't make it, that sucks, but it's just a school show, right? And there's always next year."

Gretchen nodded. "Plus, if I do make it, I'd have to tell my parents." Her hands were now twisting the paper. It looked pretty ragged. I had doubts about its survival into the audition room.

"Well, yeah," I said.

"They wouldn't like it."

"Why not?"

She gave me a "You're kidding, right, you complete and total idiot?" look. "Asian," she said, gesturing at her face.

"What? I don't know your parents. Maybe they're progressive Asians. Maybe you're adopted."

"Nope and nope."

"Maybe once you get into the show and they come see you and see how talented you are, they'll change their minds and think their daughter doing stand-up is the most awesome thing in the entire —"

Gretchen rolled her eyes so hard I expected to have to chase them across the floor and give them to her to put back in her head.

"Okay, never mind," I said.

"I'm not even supposed to be here right now," Gretchen said. "They think I'm working on my science-fair project."

"So what *are* you gonna do if you get in?"

"Cross that bridge," she said darkly.

We sat in silence for a moment. I glanced at the clock and felt myself getting nervous again.

"Just tell me your opening line," I said.

"Oh, my God, I said no already! Why don't *you* play something for me, and *then* we can talk about whether I'll —"

I was already whipping through a four-octave G scale before she even finished her sentence. It turned out flawless. I hadn't expected it to, but somehow, channeling my nervous energy into talking to Gretchen (or goading her about her act) had calmed my fingers down. My left hand was no longer jumpy. My right hand was no longer oddly stiff. I finished with a flourish that was a hair too exaggerated, but I didn't bother to feel embarrassed because it's not like she was familiar with my playing style. For all she knew, I was normally that dramatic.[4]

"Oh. That was really good," she said.

"Thanks. I'm gonna assume your act is not, then, since you won't do it." I cocked an eyebrow at her. A dare.

"I don't have to take that from a Jew," she said. Her face

4. My style has actually been described by my teacher at various times as "staid," "stoic," "zombie-like," and "Did you take a Vicodin or something?"

was deadpan, her voice neutral, but her eyes were sparkling. A challenge.

"Whatever, slanty-eyes," I answered in an equally serious tone. "Go back to the rice paddy." I mentally winced in preparation for if it didn't go over well, but —

She burst out laughing, a sound like a bell, much more delicate than the tone of her regular speaking voice. I started laughing, too, and then the door opened. "Gretchen?"

Gretchen's face froze. She made a noise that was probably meant to be "yes" but came out more like a squeak, then got up and went inside. The door closed, and for the next five minutes, all I heard was excruciating silence. No applause. No talking. Certainly no laughter. She was either whispering her entire routine and they were whispering their appreciation, or she was bombing.

Bombing *big-time.*

I was suddenly very, very nervous again.

Another long, excruciating, silent minute as I stared at the wall clock, clinging tensely to my violin, silently fingering arpeggios up and down, up and down, up and down. Finally, the door opened and she came out.

"That went well," she said with an exaggerated gesture of both arms. It took me a second to realize that not only was she being sarcastic; she was also being sarcastic *about* being sarcastic, overemphasizing the fact that she was using a cliché. It took me another second to realize that I totally did not

have time to analyze the layers of somebody else's behavior right now. Because I was next.

My heart pounded. My hands shook.

"Do you wanna go out with me sometime?" I blurted.

Gretchen laughed. The bell sound again. The first laughter I'd heard in almost ten minutes. "Ha, thanks," she said. "Okay, I feel marginally better." Then she saw my face. "Oh. You're serious."

"Yeah," I said. My voice caught in my throat halfway through, turning the end of the word into a weird gurgle. Great.

No laughs now, just a smile.

"No," she said.

"Oh." I looked down at my violin.

"I don't want to be the girl who just, like, totally screwed up her thing and feels all bad about it, so then has to get a self-esteem pick-me-up from some guy asking her out, if that makes any sense?"

"Oh," I said. "Okay. I understand." I didn't understand. I didn't see how the two things were even related, but it didn't seem like pointing any of that out was going to endear me to her.

"Nice seeing you again, though!" She flashed me a grin and was out the door.

Dammit.

They called my name. I picked up my violin and went inside.

It was as silent during my performance as it had been during Gretchen's. I was once again very, very nervous. Sweaty hands. Shaking fingers. I didn't drop anything, but let's just say the number of times I messed up the first few phrases and asked to start over was more than zero. (It was six.)

But when I came out, Gretchen was back. Sitting there. Perched in the same chair she'd been in before.

"Okay," she said. "I changed my mind. Yes."

"What?" I asked, still shell-shocked from how truly badly I'd just screwed up. An hour of practice every day for the past month, and yet . . .

"Yes, I'll go out with you sometime," she said. "Uh . . . unless . . . you changed your mind. In which case forget it, forget I said anything—" She got up, blushing a little, and started heading for the door.

"What? No! No, I mean yes—I mean no, I didn't change my mind," I said, following her. "Uh . . . why did you change yours?"

"I can't tell you that," she said. "Asians are supposed to be inscrutable, remember?"

"I don't remember," I said. "I don't know what 'inscrutable' means."

That made her smile.

And I was so pumped up, I dropped my bow, which hit the floor and broke.

And Gretchen, that tiny, cute monster, that impressively slow walker, that possibly-bad-but-possibly-just-nervous-would-be-talent-show-stand-up, laughed and picked it up for me.

Voilà!

DEBBIE RIGAUD

When I was little, my great-aunt Ma Tante used to feed me breakfast. That was when she had a straight back—so long ago, I wasn't wearing glasses yet, if you can imagine. I must have been about three. My parents were at work, my big sister at school, so it was just Ma Tante and me.

As she dipped my bread in coffee, I got distracted by tiny particles floating in the beam of light entering the window above the kitchen sink. Ma Tante, ever vigilant of my feelings, asked what I was staring at. The peanut-butter-lathered bread I had been chewing stalled in the crook of my cheek. I pointed to the snowfall of particles. It seemed like the most magical thing I'd ever seen.

Ma Tante smiled. "Magical, *non*?" she asked, echoing my thoughts. "Things are always floating around us. But just like that sunbeam, it takes the light in our hearts to see magic that is invisible to most people."

From then on, wherever I went, I searched for magic around me.

"*Voilà,*" Ma Tante would say to alert me to the tiny, every-day miracles in progress.

It was our secret.

I liked it better back when Tara and Tina were ignorant. Ever since the earthquake, this office's two medical assistants (or, as Ma Tante playfully refers to them, "the lookalikes") think they know everything about me. It's only been five minutes since my sister, Anne, dropped us off here, yet I'm already annoyed.

A sympathetic expression stretches the corners of Tara's eyes as she waits for my reply. She's taller and older than her sister.

"Yup—I'm fourteen now." I nod, squeezing the last bit of polite from my reserves. "And yes—*both* my parents are from Haiti."

"Oh, you see, TiTi?" Tara nudges her sister with the back of her hand. "I told you!"

I shrug. People have assumed this before—that I'm only half Haitian. Or at least, those who can't understand how a person with longer hair or lighter skin could come from Haiti.

My great-aunt is positioning her metal cane below her seat as she settles into her chair, getting acquainted with its contours in preparation for the long wait before her name is finally called. The doctor's office is filling up quickly. Over the past few years, as Ma Tante's painfully curved back has pulled her closer to the earth, the matching-scrub sisters started jumping her nearer to the top of the waiting list. But it's still going to take time. Lots of it.

"Go sit down, baby," Tara says, taking pity on me. "We'll call your auntie's name when the doctor is ready."

I harrumph to myself on my way to the empty seat next to Ma Tante. *When the doctor is ready.* I could bet any money he isn't even in. It never fails—halfway through our wait, the top of the good doctor's ample-sized dome can be seen bobbing past the driveway-facing window. He thinks he's sneaking in, but his conspicuously big head always gives him away.

Maybe it's because he serves the elderly. Or perhaps he's really Superman in disguise and there's always one too many emergencies going on at the local hospital. Whatever his story, Dr. Bighead's rarely in his office. Patients crowd the first floor of the converted old-time mansion that's rotting in the East Ward of our fair city. Waiting.

The one TV hanging precariously high in the corner is the waiting room's only timekeeper. Each program's theme song chimes the passing of yet another thirty minutes. From daytime talk shows to the evening news, they wait.

"Judge Judy's on," the large woman spread out over two chairs mutters to no one in particular. "Been here since *Good Morning America.*"

Ma Tante's done her share of waiting. She's been their patient—right word for sure—for over a decade. Some of my cousins are physicians, and I've heard them asking Ma Tante (on more than one occasion) to switch doctors. The old lady's too loyal to Dr. Bighead. She thinks he can do no wrong. But from where I sit, all he does is prescribe her more and more horse pills. And make her wait hours to be seen. Ma Tante doesn't speak English, so one of us waits with her. That is, until my older sister, Anne, learned to drive. The past few times, we've dropped Ma Tante off and popped in five hours later in time to translate her consultation. Not today, though. Anne dropped us *both* off, promising to be back minutes after we call her. I couldn't go home with her today because she said she had to go straight to a meeting. *Yeah, right.* Must be a really cute "study group" this time.

"*Sal' di?*" Ma Tante asks in Creole when I reach her. She wants to know what all the discussion with the lookalikes was about.

"*Rien,*" I respond respectfully—i.e., in French—as I was

raised to do when addressing an adult. I protect Ma Tante from the truth. It would hurt her to find out that, after all these years, the lookalikes have no clue that she is Haitian. Besides, Ma Tante thinks everyone adores her. And what's not to love? Most folks see this charming old lady with a peaceful gaze and a curved back and they have to restrain themselves from crouching down to hug her.

Ma Tante likes to flash her toothy smile and give away the only English offerings in her cherished possession. "Tank hyu," she answers, no matter what people say. Plus, Ma Tante treats Dr. Bighead's office like a nightclub. She dresses to the nines for her monthly appointments. Besides church, it's the only time she gets to go out these days. Today her flowery peach dress matches her hat, and she pulls an ornately embroidered handkerchief from her clutch purse.

"The lookalikes probably wanted to know where I've been," she says proudly, patting her forehead with the hankie. "They haven't seen me in a while."

"*Everybody* misses you when you're not around," I say.

She knows I'm teasing. "That's because they like how they feel about themselves when they see me," she says with that wisecracking tone in her voice.

"*Vraiment?*" I ask, a bit surprised that she's in the mood to talk. Ma Tante's obviously glad for my company—which makes me feel bad about sulking. Usually in public, she likes to keep the appearance of being a quiet, sweet old lady—not the hilarious, observant woman I enjoy being around. "Really? And why's that?"

"One look at my wrinkles, and they're excited they're not as shriveled up as me."

We tumble into a silent giggle. Me, shaking my head no and Ma Tante gesturing *oui*. But as messed up as it sounds, Ma Tante's probably right. Most people don't recognize the gems in front of them. And to me, Ma Tante is the most precious kind.

"That's not true, Ma Tante," I say, and rub her forearm, enjoying the easy movement of her loose chocolate skin. "You're a beautiful queen."

"Aaah, Simone." Ma Tante sings out my name in a delight that reveals she knew what I was thinking.

"Aaay, Simone?" This time my name rings out from a deeper voice. "Simone Thibodeaux?"

The first thing that catches my eye is his T-shirt. It's blue like his jeans, but with bright-orange letters that grab me. It reads CARE-A-VAN and under that, *Transporting Seniors to Caregivers.* The brain works superhero-fast. Quicker than an eye blink, I recognize the name of the volunteer group kids at my school sign up for in a frenzy to reach their monthly community service quota. Another millisecond later, my eyes dart up to the shirt wearer's face. What's Louis Milton doing way over in *this* part of town? He's from the West Ward.

"You're a volunteer here, too?" he asks.

"Um, no," I mutter, suddenly self-conscious. I clutch my phone. Why did Anne have to dump me here *today*?

"Oh," he says, and I can see he understands. *You're from the East Ward.* Before I can busy myself with a fake text, he continues. "Nice running into you, though."

I recognize that sympathetic look. I've seen it every time I have to turn down my friends because my parents won't let me go all the way to the West Ward at night. I hate that he feels sorry for me.

"Louis, help me out here, will you?" a girl calls from the front door. Oh, great. It's Waverly Webber from my history class. She's struggling to get an elderly man's wheelchair through the narrow entrance.

"Excuse me," Louis says to me before jogging over and pinning the heavy door wide open. Once Waverly and her senior are safely inside, Louis slips out.

"Gotcha here in one piece, Mr. P.," Waverly announces proudly.

Perhaps it's the piercing voice or the shift in the air brought on by Waverly's mere presence, but Ma Tante opens her heavy eyes wide and looks my classmate up and down.

"*Sal' yé?*" Ma Tante sings out under her breath, basically asking WTF (minus the F) in Creole.

Funny how Ma Tante picks up in Waverly what I do. The girl's actually never been mean to me or anyone else I know. It's just that her "Me first!" vibe can be off-putting.

This office never looked terribly low-budget to me before. But now, seeing Waverly here — her velvet red ballet flats stepping on aged, peeling linoleum floors — it's hard not to view things through her eyes. I suddenly feel exposed, as if Waverly just walked in on me getting my hair braided.

Good thing she doesn't notice me. Waverly's busying herself to our left, rearranging chairs to make room for her elderly companion's wheelchair. As she jams it into a narrow spot, the rush of the empty row of chairs slams Ma Tante's seat into mine.

Ma Tante reacts quietly. "Oh-oh?"

Mr. P. checks his neck for whiplash.

"There you *go*," Waverly tells him, smiling. She wipes her palms against each other and reports to the front desk in three quick strides. "I've brought Charles Pemberton for his three o'clock appointment."

If only Waverly knew that to Dr. Bighead, three p.m. means seven or eight p.m.

"Oh, and here's a list of medications that Mr. P. is currently taking," she says, not missing a beat.

"Okay, baby," Tina, the younger lookalike, says, taking the sheet from Waverly. "When the doctor comes in, we'll give this list to him."

The astonished look that takes hold of Waverly's face is priceless. "You mean he isn't here yet?"

Ma Tante pauses her humming to give a quiet chuckle.

"He'll be here soon enough," Tina says dismissively before heading toward the break room.

Perplexed, Waverly stops short of scratching her head when she spots me. "What're *you* doing here, Simone?"

"Hey, Waverly." I don't answer her question. This is my second chance to introduce Ma Tante, but I don't take it. I feel bad about that, but my embarrassment at being seen in the ghetto doctor's office outweighs the guilt.

But Waverly can't be shaken off the trail that easily. "Is this your grandmother?" she asks. Then to Ma Tante: "Hello, I'm Waverly — I go to school with your granddaughter."

"Mhmm. Tank hyu." Ma Tante smiles politely.

"She speaks Haitian?" Waverly asks, obviously tickled by Ma Tante's accent.

"Creole," I correct her. "And French."

Waverly finally asks her burning question. "So, you're here . . . even though you don't get any school credit for it?"

I nod. "I think they have new patient forms for the man you came in with," I say, counting on the fact that Waverly hates to miss a step.

It works. Her lips form an O, and she pads over to grab a clipboard.

Louis comes back, escorting a woman who walks with a cane. He looks so gentlemanly with his elbow extended for her to hold. A celebrated football player at school, Louis is taller and bigger than the average guy his age — so I'm mesmerized by how much he outsizes his companion.

The elderly woman lets go of Louis's arm and excitedly waves at Ma Tante. *"Koman ou ye?"*

"Oh!" Ma Tante sits up as best she can. *"Madame Bertrand, koman ou ye?"*

Louis seems touched by the women's gleeful greetings. His round face lights up like a stadium scoreboard at one of his home games. Despite his bulk, Louis is delicate with Madame Bertrand as he helps her into the seat next to Ma Tante's.

I get up to kiss Ma Tante's friend on the cheek. Even though I've never met her, doing so is customary. I stay standing. Here's my chance to redeem myself.

"Uh, Louis, this is my great-aunt, Ma Tante," I say.

Louis respectfully takes off his baseball cap and shakes Ma Tante's hand. He doesn't know about the cheek kiss custom, so he gets a pass.

"Janti ti gason." Ma Tante is impressed with him.

"Eh-heh." Madame Bertrand accepts the compliment as if Louis is her grandson.

"He would make a nice friend for my Simone," Ma Tante continues in Creole.

"I think so, too," replies Madame Bertrand.

"It's cute how they steal glances at each other, *non*?"

I can't hide my surprise, and Louis takes notice.

"What are they saying?" he asks me.

"Uh," I pause. "Just that . . . you're a well-mannered young man."

"Did he just ask you on a date, Simone?" Ma Tante is really trying to mess with me now.

"I'm going to have to separate you two," I answer, sassy in Creole.

The women giggle over Louis's confusion.

"I think they're saying more than that," he says, laughing and scanning all of our faces for clues. "C'mon, Simone, you're holding back."

"Simone, are you translating for Louis?" Waverly's finished Mr. P.'s paperwork and is drawn in by our laughter.

"Something like that," I answer, still blushing.

Waverly has an epiphany. "You can totally get credit for translating for Care-A-Van," she says earnestly. "Some Haitian seniors in the program need translators."

You know what? That could be cool. "That would be cool," I say.

"I'll introduce you to the program director, and you can get started right away," Waverly offers.

Funny that her persistence feels a lot more bearable when it benefits me.

"April Johnson?" Tara calls a patient to the back. Finally.

The large woman using two seats gets up, sighs heavily, and waddles to the exam room.

Immediately, Mr. P. rises effortlessly from the wheelchair and strides to nab the now vacant best seat in the house for TV viewing. We all look on in stunned silence.

"I told that chile I ain't need to be *wheeled* in," Mr. P. grumbles.

Ma Tante and I look at each other and burst out laughing. Louis, Madame Bertrand, and eventually even Waverly and Mr. P., cackle heartily with us.

"Voilà." Ma Tante winks at me.

I wink back.

THREE-POINTER

MITALI PERKINS

I have two gorgeous older sisters, but let the record stand: I was the first Bose daughter to score a point in the Game of Guys.

His name? Dwayne.

The place? A playground across the street from our Flushing, Queens, apartment, where I'd swing, slide, and ride my bike along with hordes of other immigrant kids.

The technique? Dwayne screeched his two-wheeler to a halt in front of mine, patted his Jackson Five Afro, and said, "Going to White Castle for lunch. Want to come along?"

Dumbstruck, I shook my head shyly and biked away.

I was nine.

Looking back, I should have eagerly accepted: "Yes, Dwayne, I'll go to White Castle with you. And then you're taking me to the prom in a decade or so, got that?"

It would be the only romantic invitation I'd get for years.

Soon after Dwayne made his move, our family left New York and settled in a San Francisco Bay Area suburb. I was in middle school, and my sisters were almost done with high school. Sonali, the oldest (her name means "gold" in Bangla), was a numbers geek, and Rupali ("silver") was an outgoing, leader-of-the-pack type. I came third ("friendly" — more valuable than precious metals in the long run, mind you), and my face was constantly planted in fiction. We Bose girls were nothing alike, but here's what we had in common: all of us liked guys. It was so much fun to watch, crush on, and, we hoped, date them.

The only problem was that we were the first Indians to move into this California neighborhood. In fact, we were the only folk of Asian descent for miles around. Also, there were no signs of any Afros like Dwayne's. The sea of whiteness didn't hinder my sisters — turned out plenty of Bay Area college dudes wanted tropical teen arm candy to complement their hippie lifestyles. Sonali and Rupali quickly ascended to expert level in the Guy Game.

Our parents knew nothing about this pursuit — they planned to arrange our marriages to suitable Indian men once we graduated with appropriate degrees in engineering or biology. Their ignorance was our bliss, we decided, especially when it came to dating. I kept my sisters' secrets, but I also secretly kept score. A sibling got one point if someone asked her out. A second if he gave her a compliment. A quick kiss won her a third. That's as far as I counted — going after a fourth point with the same guy would put my sisters in territory too dangerous to fathom. Heck, I figured if Baba caught them winning even one point, they'd be shipped to Kolkata and paraded before a bunch of parentally approved prospective grooms. Thankfully, Ma and Baba stayed out of the loop, and my sisters continued to accrue points right and left.

Sadly, when it came to me, Dwayne's invitation was still my only score. And it didn't seem like that was going to change too soon. At first, the other middle-schoolers in this born-in-the-USA neighborhood didn't know what to do with me. A few mumbled "hey" from a safe distance; most totally ignored my existence.

I didn't get why I immediately ranked so low on the social ladder, but in retrospect it's not hard to figure out. I would have crushed the competition in a Fresh Off the Boat poster contest. I was the whole FOB package — parents with lilting accents, super-strict father who didn't accept grades less than an A, house that perpetually smelled like turmeric and cardamom, ultra-traditional mother whose idea of party garb was six-and-a-half yards of silk *saree* and a forehead dot that mesmerized our neighbors. Plus, my skin was a color writers usually describe with food products like chocolate and coffee. At least *my* metaphors were addictive and tasty, right? I found it harder to define my classmates' hues in my diary.

They certainly weren't milky white, but "skin like deli-sliced turkey" didn't sound too appealing.

Surprisingly, the second time I gave myself a point in the game came after a few long weeks of peer-group silence. At lunch one day, a group of five geeks approached me. (You know the kind—precursors to today's *Lord of the Rings* fans who still collect Pokémon cards by the time they get to college.) My '70s geeks stood silently for a few minutes, elbowing one another to speak. One finally gathered his courage. "We need an Uhura," he told me. "We're heading to our usual spot over there. Want to come along?" The others nodded and waited eagerly for my answer.

I had no idea what they were talking about. After some questioning, I discovered these were Trekkies of a most intense type. They reenacted episodes of *Star Trek* every day in their corner of the cafeteria, each taking the role of a male character in the six-person cast. The sixth character in the show was a brown girl named Uhura, and it was clear (to them) that I'd been beamed down to repeat her few but important lines. I considered the invitation briefly—Spock was hot—before crushing their hopes.

The remainder of middle school involved episodes like a painful social dance class in PE, where I overheard a popular guy muttering about "fox-trotting with the Unibrow."

Mortified, I ran home to the bathroom mirror. Sure enough, my eyebrows were as impermeable as the fence between California and Mexico. My forehead was in San Diego, and my eyes were in Tijuana. My sisters found me in the bathroom crying over my hirsutism (look it up: excessive hairiness is a real diagnosis) and decided I needed help.

Rupali introduced me to eyeliner, tweezers, and a range of facial-hair removal strategies. Turned out American beauty products can take the South Asian right out of a girl.

Sonali excelled in science, so she told me about sex.

"You mean I won't get pregnant while using a public toilet?" I asked. That had been one of Ma's no-sex tips, filed under the broader category of "Avoid all contact with boys." "What about swimming at the Y?"

"Nope," my sister said. "The Y pool is pretty much baby-free. That is, if a girl keeps her suit on. Here, let me draw some pictures."

After digesting the facts of life as explained by my A+-in-biology sister, I pondered the miracle of our existence. Ma and Baba never touched in public or in front of us. The thought of either of them taking off any clothing was unimaginable. How in the world had the three of us been conceived through yards and yards of *saree* fabric?

My sisters' point totals were climbing, and I spied constantly on their dates (which usually started once the three of us were at the mall). I noticed two nonverbals that could come in handy if opportunity ever came my way: the Smoldering Look and the Hair Twiddle. Apparently, combining the two at the right time could seal the deal. I practiced for hours in front of the bathroom mirror.

Thanks to this intense sisterly schooling, I began to relax around guys. I even made some male friends by the time I started high school. These buddies confessed crushes on other girls in excruciating detail, and in return I offered advice gleaned from the adult fiction section of the library. Well-researched romance novels soon turned me into the school's number-one dating guru. I was at a suburban high school wearing jeans, not perched on a mountaintop in a white *saree*, but it didn't matter — scores of young men streamed to me for relationship advice.

No new points, though.

Meanwhile, my sisters suddenly stopped playing altogether. Thanks to a blossoming feminist movement on their college campus and a bunch of not-so-great experiences, they were now bemoaning time wasted with Stone Age chauvinists and losers masquerading as good guys. *Learn from our mistakes,* they warned me. *Wait for quality; skip the quantity.* I listened (sort of) but couldn't help thinking it was fine for them to quit, but I was still only at a grand total of two points. And did Dwayne's playground invitation and Spock's geeky move even count?

Then Steve moved into the neighborhood. He was a basketball star with strawberry-blond hair and blue eyes, so gorgeous that girls finger-fanned their faces when discussing him in the locker room. On his first day at school, I watched him open a door for a tottering, seventy-something history teacher, and *bam*, I was gone.

Steve turned up in most of my honors classes, and I put my best "I'm your buddy" foot forward. It worked superbly. After we shared a laugh or two, it was easy to add him to my coterie of guy friends. On the outside, that is. On the inside, I crushed on him madly, from freshman year until junior year. Nobody knew and nobody asked. I told the truth only to my diary, an orange notebook stashed deep in my desk.

By junior year, I was losing hope. There was no way Steve was going to like me. Not in that way, not a chance. I'd seen the vacancy in my male friends' eyes as they skipped across my face and body to scan a room for their white crushes. I did have the necessary feminine equipment, don't get me wrong, but apparently my body parts were the wrong hue to hold a gaze. In this neighborhood, they preferred deli-sliced turkey.

And then it happened. Steve stopped at our table on the way to eat with his basketball buddies. I was sitting with three of my friends, pretty Brady Bunch–ish blondes munching on PB & Js. Usually, guys talked to me with eyes fixed on my companions, but Steve was looking at me. Only me. And he was standing closer than any male buddy ever had. "Like roller coasters, Mitali?" he asked.

Swallowing the bite of leftover lentils and rice Ma had packed for me, I prayed he couldn't smell mango pickle on my breath. "Love them," I said, smiling brightly. *You've never ridden a roller coaster, you idiot. Don't lie to him!* "Love the idea of them, I mean. I've never tried one in real life."

"What?" asked Marcia, Jan, and Cindy in unison.

"Are you joking?"

"Don't they have roller coasters in India?"

Maybe they did. But we'd left before I had a chance to find out. Besides, life in a suburban American school felt like a crazy thrill ride that never ended. Who needed the real thing?

"You'll like the Giant Dipper," Steve said. "Our church youth group is heading to Santa Cruz on Saturday. Want to come along?"

Want to come along? I could hardly believe it — my dream guy had just joined the short list of dudes to ask me that question. First Dwayne, then Spock, and now . . . Steve. Apparently, I scored points only at lunch. "Sure," I said, deploying two years of finely honed "I'm your friend" acting skills to keep from shouting the word.

"We'll pick you up at noon," he said. "What's your address?"

"Sounds great," I said, lying again as I scribbled my address on a napkin. How would I explain a ginger-headed basketball player to my blissfully ignorant parents? Once again, I'd have to enlist my sisters' mad skills.

Steve tucked the napkin into his pocket and moved on. The girls at my table were quiet, but only for a bit. I watched them shake it off and start to chat about their weekend plans. This invitation was a blip, for sure. Guys asked *them* out in front of *me*, not vice versa. When it came to the scripts of their lives, I was the fourth chick, the one without a speaking part, the sidekick who never got her own backstory. I was starting to suspect I was only in the movie so the protagonist could add dimension to her character.

Saturday dawned, a breezy, summery, Santa Cruz–perfect day. I knew it wasn't a real date—there were a bunch of us going—but he had asked *me*, right?

"Are you sure this jock is worth it?" Sonali asked doubtfully.

Rupali chimed in. "Why's it taken him so long to ask you out?"

I didn't answer. My sisters exchanged glances and shrugged.

"Let's get you ready," said Rupali.

"What's our game plan?" asked Sonali.

I tried on eleven outfits before they finally agreed on the perfect combination—faded jeans, a white cotton shirt embroidered with flowers, and sandals with bling. Rupali convinced Ma to go shopping, Sonali asked Baba for help in chemistry, and I stole out to the porch to wait. My sisters were going to tell the truncated truth—I was spending the day at a park with some nice, studious friends.

The church ride was on time. I dashed to the curb and

jumped in before Steve had a chance to get out or Baba glanced up from Sonali's chemistry textbook. Acquaintances from school jammed the car, so no introductions were needed. We chatted with the others on the drive, but once we got into the amusement park, Steve led me away from the group.

"See you in a while," he told them, leaving a wake of confusion behind us. *Why does HE want to be alone with HER?* I could hear them thinking.

Before I could ask myself the same question, we were standing by the Giant Dipper. It was white, wooden, rickety, and huge. I gulped. "You'll like it—I promise," Steve said. "Just don't fight it."

He was right—I loved it. My head buzzed with the nearness of him as the Dipper twisted and turned us. That sweet old coaster kept tossing me over to Steve and hurling Steve over to me. We rode it three times, then crashed into each other's bumper cars, made crazy faces in the hall of mirrors, and shared fried dough. Steve swished a basket in the arcade and won an enormous stuffed monkey. He handed his prize to me with a smile sweeter than the dough we'd devoured.

"Let's name him Dipper," I said, swinging the huge creature onto my shoulders.

Steve reached over to brush the hair out of my eyes, and suddenly, it was time. I took a deep breath and hit him bang in the face with my best Smoldering Look. Oh, his eyes were blue, as blue as the California sky above our heads, as blue as the Pacific waves crashing on the sand. *Stow it,* I told myself. *Write the poem later. This is now, baby. Twiddle some Hair and keep Smoldering.* Oh, I Smoldered, all right. And Twiddled. All while balancing a monkey, no less — go on, try it, it's harder than it sounds — but thanks to my sisters' stellar training, I managed it.

During the ride home, Michael Jackson's "Rockin' Robin" may have been belting out on the radio, but my heart was dancing a crazy Bollywood dance. The only thing separating us was Dipper, one leg draped across Steve's jeans and one leg on mine. One by one the others were dropped off, but when it was just me and Steve in the backseat, he didn't move away. No, he stayed close, one denim leg pressed against mine. *To balance Dipper,* I thought. But then he wielded his own nonverbal. It was a classic guy move I'd watched college dudes use on my sisters: a yawn, a stretch, and suddenly an arm was stretched out across the seat behind me.

I knew the right response: lean in a little closer and clutch Dipper's paw.

The church car stopped in front of my house (*too soon, too soon*). I opened the door and swung out a leg. "Thanks so much," I said.

In a quick move, as smooth and agile as though he'd

practiced it a hundred times in front of a mirror, he leaned over and kissed my cheek. "You're sweet, Mitali," he said, and handed me the monkey.

And like that, he was gone. The car whisked him away, leaving me with points one, two, and three. I stood on the curb, squeezing Dipper so hard a real animal would have been asphyxiated in seconds. *So, that's the game,* I thought. *Hmm . . .*

The door opened. It was Ma, calling me inside, scolding about how late I was. I didn't care. I'd played the game; that was enough. But how was I going to explain the monkey business?

Like Me

VARIAN JOHNSON

"Griff, snap out of it," Evan says, jabbing his elbow into my rib cage. "You're missing the newbies."

I glance at Evan — trying to ignore the scraggly reddish-brown "soul patch" on his chin — then turn to follow his gaze. A mob of girls, huddled together like starry-eyed lambs heading to the slaughter, make their way across the quad with Principal Greer herding them along. With their blinding-white blouses and heavily starched skirts, they look like rejects from an episode of *Gossip Girl*.

Of course, my blazer and slacks would fit in the show just fine. As Principal Greer says, we're all cut from the same cloth here.

"Where are the boys? Did their group already pass?" Callie sports the same uniform as every other girl at Hobbs, but takes a more . . . generous interpretation on the skirt's length requirements.

"Did we look that scared last year?" Rebecca asks. "They're terrified."

Though talking to the group, she leans into me. I try to ignore the sweetness of her citrus-scented perfume, the color of her perfectly pink lips, the touch of her freckled hand against mine.

"Which one do you think'll bite the dust first?" Evan asks. "My bet's on the chubby one with the splotchy cheeks."

"No way," Callie says. "You see Tinkerbell — the one with the pixie cut? She probably still wets the bed."

Only a handful of events are certain at Hobbs Academy. The chicken enchilada will give you diarrhea. Coach Hawkins will mutter something inappropriate during the Spring Pep Rally and we'll all hear it thanks to the state-of-the-art sound system. And at least one freshman won't make it past the first two weeks. That last one may as well be chiseled in stone.

While Rebecca yells at Evan and Callie for being mean, my gaze falls to two girls at the tail of the mob. Rail-thin. Leggy. Dark-brown skin. Short, bouncy, black hair.

Twins? Maybe.

Black. Definitely.

I should know.

"What do you think?" Evan elbows me again, pushing me into Rebecca. "Which one leaves first?"

"The blonde," I mumble, trying to regain my balance.

"Which one?" he asks. "There are, like, twenty of them."

Exactly.

With about thirty students per grade, Hobbs is the smallest boarding school in Vermont. Our demographics are just like the state's. White, white, and white.

I guess that's not fair. Technically Rebecca is "one-eighth German, three-eighths Sephardic-Jewish, and one-half Irish." And Evan has enough Muskogee blood running through him to be a member of the Creek Nation. Still, I didn't see anyone looking at them when we talked about the Holocaust or the Trail of Tears last year in World History. But let anyone mention Dr. Martin Luther King Jr. or Will Smith or even the slightly black-looking dude who trims Principal Greer's prized rosebushes, and suddenly I'm the center of attention.

It got bad during Black History Month.

I own February at Hobbs.

Even the cafeteria lady gets in on it. Like: *I'm sorry, Griffin. So sorry. First — well, I'm sure I don't have to tell you, do I now? — we had slavery. Next came those horrible Jim Crow laws. And then Hurricane Katrina — can you believe it? Here, take an extra slice of cake. It's lemon. I've got watermelon and fried chicken and red Kool-Aid in back, too, just for you.*

(Okay, she didn't say all of that stuff. Not at the same time, anyway.)

But this afternoon in September, the cafeteria lady barely looks in my direction as she plops a scoop of lasagna onto my tray.

"Dude," Evan says as I near the table. "I heard there's twins in the new class. Twins!"

I slide into the chair beside him, bypassing the empty seat by Rebecca.

"They're in my PE class," Callie says. "Violet and Jasmine Harris. I think Coach is going to talk to them about playing volleyball."

"Volleyball-playing twins." Evan's eyes make him look like a rat in search of cheese. "How do they look?"

Callie glances at me. "You know . . . they're tall. And they have . . . brown eyes."

Evan's eyes dart around the room. "Yeah? And?"

"They're um . . . um . . ."

I drop my fork on the tray, not expecting the clang of metal on plastic to ring so loudly. "They're black."

The table falls silent. Another rule at Hobbs—no one talks about race. Like last year's mono outbreak and Principal Greer's BO, we ignore it—pretend it doesn't exist. Pretend it doesn't matter. "I saw them in the library." Rebecca picks at her salad—a sea of iceberg lettuce and creamy ranch dressing, with a few walnuts on top to make it reasonably healthy. "What makes you think they want to play volleyball?"

The question hangs in the air.

We remain statues.

Callie finally shifts. "They seemed interested in gym class." She tugs at the necklace around her reddening neck. "And I think I overheard them saying something about how they used to play at their old school."

The way she speaks, low and mumbling and more to the table than us, doesn't do her any favors.

Now it's Rebecca's turn to glance in my direction. "Callie, don't make stuff up." They've been friends since nursery school, so she never holds back.

I stare at her, and with my eyes I yell: *Control-Alt-Delete! Control-Alt-Delete!*

Rebecca doesn't get my silent code. But then again, she's a Mac type of girl. Those commands don't exist in her universe. "You thought they'd be good at sports because they're African-American. Admit it."

Callie shakes her head. "I never . . . Why would I—?"

I plaster the biggest smile I can muster to my face. "Like Callie would ever think something like that. You guys have seen me play basketball, right? Two-legged cockroaches jump higher than me."

They all laugh. Quietly. Politely.

Nothing like the way my cousins laughed when Benji cracked the same lame joke about me this summer.

Once everyone's provided the appropriate amount of laughter, we stuff whatever remains on our trays into our mouths.

Rebecca steals a few more glances at me but doesn't speak.

And Evan spends the rest of lunch talking about Tinkerbell.

So much for volleyball-playing twins.

The next day, right after calculus, I see the Harris twins coming down the hallway. Buds in their ears, heads bouncing. They're almost as tall as me, and I'm a hair under six foot.

I pause, letting everyone else slide past me out of class. When the twins are close enough, I try to catch their gaze, to give them a head nod — quick tilt back, chin up.

They keep walking. Don't even look in my direction.

Maybe they're too busy listening to their iPods.

Maybe they're too busy thinking about their next class.

Or maybe I just blend in with everyone else.

I see them a few other times over the next couple of days, sometimes in the hallway, sometimes in the caf, but I never have the opportunity to speak. I mean, yes, I *could* speak to them, but what am I supposed to say? *Hello, my Negro friends. Welcome to Hobbs Academy, which is whiter than rice and eggshells and vanilla-flavored milk. If you act like Bryant Gumbel and Wayne Brady, you'll fit right in.*

(My modification of yet another series of lame jokes about me, courtesy of Benji. Uttered anytime I walked, spoke, breathed, or blinked.)

So I don't speak to the Harris girls. And they don't speak to me. We just pass each other, day after day.

It's quite possible that I could have gone on avoiding Violet and Jasmine for another week, or maybe forever, if Rebecca hadn't called me out.

"They asked about you," she says one Thursday night when we're doing our homework in the study room on her floor. Boys are allowed on the floor until eight p.m. I've been here every night this week, even on days I didn't have homework. It's like I can't help myself.

"Who?" I ask, playing dumb.

"Violet and Jasmine."

"Oh. What did they want to know?"

"Just your name. Where you were from. If you were 'cool.'"

"Why'd they ask you?" I know the words come out harder than they're supposed to, but I need to know.

"Violet thought . . ." Rebecca flips a page in her chemistry book. "They see us together a lot."

We don't speak for a few minutes. I move on to my next calculus problem, but I may as well be deciphering Sanskrit.

It doesn't help that Rebecca's wearing her hair like she did on our trip to New York last year. The drama club went to see *Wicked* on Broadway—and even though I was a set designer (well, more like a grunt for the set designer), I got to tag along. The play was okay, I guess. All I remember is Rebecca sitting beside me, dark curls spilling over her shoulders, skin smelling like oranges and mangoes, thigh pressed against mine during the entire show.

The musical was named right. There had been something wicked going on in my head. And in my pants.

"The young twin has a boyfriend," Rebecca says. "But not the older one. Not Violet."

"Um . . . okay."

Another flip of the page. "You know . . . in case you were interested."

I shake my head harder than necessary. "I don't like her," I say. Loudly. Just to be sure she hears me. "Not like that, anyway. I don't even know her."

Rebecca shrugs. Opens her mouth. Closes it. Shrugs again. Shuts her book. Takes a breath. "You said you were going to call this summer."

Her voice is low, and the hurt on her face slams into me harder than a thousand of Benji's lame, flat, painful, offensive jokes.

"I know. I'm sorry."

"Is it because . . . ?" Whatever bravery she exhibited confronting Callie on the first day of school has withered away.

"It's because I'm stupid."

We're both quiet. Rebecca's hair falls over her face, hiding her full, round cheeks. "You should talk to them," she says softly. "They're lonely."

Now it's my turn to shrug.

The next day I head for the library, hall pass in hand. Rebecca stands at the circulation desk but busies herself by looking in every possible direction except mine.

It doesn't take me long to find Violet.

At least, I assume it's Violet. They are twins, after all.

"Violet?" I ask, nearing the table.

She looks up from her textbook and slips the buds from her ears. "Griff. Wassup."

I sit down across from her. Her skin glows under the hard, bright fluorescent lights. "I just wanted to officially introduce myself. I've been meaning to, but —"

"Don't sweat it. I'm sure you got better things to do than hang with someone like me."

The sweat collecting underneath my arms approaches oceanic levels. "What makes you think that?"

"I'm a freshman. Low man on the totem pole."

"Sophomores aren't much better off," I mumble. "So where's your sister?"

Her smile falters. "In study hall, texting that sorry, trifling boyfriend of hers." She leans closer to me. She smells like aloe vera. Nice, but nothing like citrus. "I miss my boyfriend, too, but you don't see me moping around."

She has a boyfriend. I want to turn toward Rebecca and her dark curls and citrus-scented skin and yell, *She has a boyfriend!*

"It ain't just him. It's home." She strums the table. "She misses home."

"Hobbs takes a while to get used to."

"How long did it take you?"

I laugh. "When I get there, I'll let you know."

I'm in the middle of telling her about what cafeteria meals to avoid when Mrs. Whittaker walks over. The school librarian is out on maternity leave, so Mandy Whittaker's mom offered to substitute. Like an English degree, two snobby teens, and a huge bank account make you an expert on all things literary.

"You two getting any work done?" Mrs. Whittaker asks.

"Griffin was nice enough to come over and introduce himself. He's giving me some pointers about school."

She glances at Violet's notebook. "What are you studying?"

"English." She moves her hand, giving Mrs. Whittaker

full view of her notebook. "I'm working on an essay on *I Know Why the Caged Bird Sings. By Maya Angelou.*"

"I'm familiar with the book," Mrs. Whittaker says, touching the top button of her blouse. "I thought your class was reading *The Book Thief.*"

"By Markus Zusak. I read it last year." She doesn't blink an eye. "Mr. Brooks and I thought it would be more worthwhile to focus on another book."

"I see." Mrs. Whittaker's voice is different. Smaller. She looks around the table, letting her eyes settle on the open Angelou book. The pages sport an assortment of highlights and underlines, with notes in the margins.

"It's my personal copy," Violet says.

"Of course." Mrs. Whittaker nods to Violet, then to me. "Let me know if I can help, okay?"

After Mrs. Whittaker leaves, Violet shakes her head. Her eyes remind me of a dull penny. "Sorry 'bout getting you into trouble. My bad."

It's almost magical, the way she switches talking like that.

Some people call it slang.

Teachers call it bad English.

Idiots call it Ebonics.

And me—I call it just talking. Like you do with family.

I want to be like her, loose and carefree with my vowels and consonants, right here at Hobbs. Because lately, even at home with my cousins, the words are starting to come out stiff and broken and wrong. The last time I was home, they said I sounded white.

I shake this thought away. "I'm not worried about Mrs. Whittaker."

"That ain't who I'm talking about."

I look back toward the circulation desk. Rebecca is scrubbing the counter with a dust rag. I can almost see the varnish rising from the counter, and the steam rising from her head.

"She don't have anything to worry about. Like I said, I have a boyfriend." She glances at Rebecca. "She's nice. Everybody thinks you two would make a nice couple."

"Really?" I ask. "Everyone?"

The way she looks at me, I know she understands what I'm trying to ask.

"Don't date her if you don't want to. It's a free country. But she's got it bad for you. And from the way it sounds, you're jonesing for her, too."

That's all she says. No jokes about the other white meat. No teasing about the black man's kryptonite. No jabs about Mr. Oreo looking for a glass of milk.

She picks up her earbuds. "I'd better get back to work. This essay ain't going to write itself."

I take a scrap of paper and scribble my number on it. "Just in case you need to get ahold of me. About anything."

She takes the paper. "Hey, whatcha got going on this weekend? Want to hang out with me and Jazzy on Saturday? It might take her mind off of home and that sorry boyfriend of hers." She pops her knuckles. "I've been waiting for the right time to bring out the dominoes. And now that we have a third player . . ."

I think about lying or coming up with some excuse, but after the conversation we had, Violet deserves better. "I don't know how to play."

She blinks twice, like she's processing the data. "Oh. Okay. We'll teach you."

I sit there, not sure what to say.

She's already got her nose back in her book. "And if you want, bring Rebecca. That way we can play spades, too."

I head to circulation, which smells of wildflowers and ammonia. And oranges and mangoes. "Thanks for getting me to talk to Violet."

"No problem. I forgot you guys were even in here."

Sure she did. I reach across the wide desk and place my hand on hers. Mrs. Whittaker would have a heart attack if she saw, but who cares? "What are you doing for lunch?"

She glances at my hand. "You don't want to go to the caf with Evan and Callie?"

"No. Let's walk over to Pat's."

"Just us?"

"Yeah. Just us. Like we used to last year."

She gives me a smile that grabs me and refuses to let go. "You're buying."

I squeeze her hand, smile one last time, and head for the exit. Right before I open the door, I look back at Violet and give her a head nod.

She sees me, and she nods back.

Confessions of a Black Geek

OLUGBEMISOLA RHUDAY-PERKOVICH

In high school, my friends and I owned two words — we were Black, and we were geeks. We had the soundtrack to prove the first: classic Nina Simone and Aretha Franklin renditions of "Young, Gifted and Black." That song was as much a part of my regular diet as the lumpy and not-sweet-enough porridge I had for breakfast many mornings. My mom was an Excellence for Black Children mother, which meant that she battled for Parent-of-a-High-Achiever supremacy at monthly meetings and was quick to whip out the dashiki and boom box so that I could dance interpretively alongside my equally gifted and well-mothered friends at the annual Martin Luther King Jr. breakfasts.

We were on display at family gatherings, too — some evil auntie or uncle got the idea to have "the young people" perform every Thanksgiving before dinner. If we did not slouch to the center of the living room to recite a little Langston Hughes or perform a painful excerpt from our last piano recital, we could forget about eating. My cousins and I grumbled and threatened revolt, but . . . miss out on more codfish cakes and mac and cheese? We performed.

But let's be honest. My friends and I didn't need *that* much prodding to put excellence on display, especially the academic variety. We were serious geeks. Second proof: we voluntarily joined (and were the only members of) the math and debate teams. We brought *all* of our textbooks home daily (just in case) in book bags the size of igloos. K. and I would call each other breathlessly on report card day to tally our As and A+s. (It was understood that the occasional B was too devastating to discuss.) We took such excessive pride in our academic achievements that when K. received an A instead of an A+ with a 98 average, we hurried to Mrs. H. to rectify this grievous error, with me along as his consigliere. Maybe Mrs. H. had gotten confused?

No. The A would stand, "because you're pompous," she told us.

Okay, so Mrs. H. wasn't confused. But clearly she needed a sabbatical.

Looking back, though, Mrs. H. might have been onto something. K. and I *were* certain that our all-around fabulos-ity knew no bounds, and certainly not racial ones. Our high school was an oasis of suburban racial integration. These were the '80s; "Ebony and Ivory," Stevie Wonder and Paul McCartney's pop hit of the era, could have been our school song. Jheri-curled and Sun-In'd hairstyles were equally welcome at the best parties. Our school put on *The Wiz* with a multiracial cast, and when we did *The Crucible,* the drama coach was sensitive enough to ask the Black members of the troupe if we'd be uncomfortable playing the role of slave Tituba. "Ummmm . . . yeah," I murmured, imagining my mother's face if I'd dared to come home saying, "Hey, Mom! I'm going to play the slave in the school play! Invite the whole family!" She would've thought I'd lost my mind.

Still, I was secure enough in my two-word identity to wear different personas like the rubber bracelets that snaked up my arms. In playwriting workshop, I explored my younger days of dancing on the bed with a "blond" towel on my head in a thoughtful piece; after school, I giggled through the mall talking like a Valley girl with friends of every shape, size, and hue—we were like piano keys, melodious and harmonic, dancing to the same beat of mutual respect. We acknowledged the chocolate-and-peanut-butter perfection of Aerosmith and Run-D.M.C on "Walk This Way." Smurf was both TV noun and dance-party verb, and Prince vs. Michael Jackson? Stumped us all. Just when *Thriller* and the moonwalk took our collective breath away, *Purple Rain* stormed in, wearing high-heeled boots and rolling pop, rock, heavy metal, and

R&B into a glorious ball of awesome. Black and White, we all loved the spare beats and synthesizers of '80s music (and the hair! Have you *seen* the *hair*? Seriously, google it. I'll wait.).

So of course, my friends and I were sure our White classmates weren't *racist*. Racists were red-faced people wearing white sheets. They were not sitting next to us in AP English or competing with us for the Individual Research Projects in Science Award. We giggled and got good grades alongside one another, we were on the honor roll together, and we collectively celebrated the rise of hip-hop and blue-eyed soul.

But surface harmony notwithstanding, there were cracks in the veneer.

When I proudly displayed one of Keith Haring's giant Free South Africa posters in my room, a friend came to visit and went white with outrage (pun intended). "That poster seems like it's saying the Black people should rise up and crush White people," he said. "They should really *try talking to them first.*"

Of course.

The nearly fifty years of resistance to the government system of apartheid could not have possibly included some talking.

Even the music we shared started to feel a bit offbeat. As much as I admired the philanthropic sentiment, some of the lyrics in "Do They Know It's Christmas?" the star-studded musical call for famine relief in Ethiopia, made me squirm.

At school assemblies, the whole student body rapped and sang along to "Caravan of Love" and "King Holiday," but the ugliness of Howard Beach, where a group of Black men were chased by a mob of White men through the streets of New York City and severely beaten, was only minutes away.

My visits to the school library stopped after I'd asked the librarian where I might find resources for my research paper on Zora Neale Hurston and she told me there was "no such person."

Oh-kayy . . .

Whatever. I had work to do. I was getting ready to move on to college, where surely more enlightened adults waited to affirm my brilliance. Pompous, that's right.

Then the school newspaper published a cartoon featuring Black teens speaking "Ebonically" ("Dat's nasty!"). My friends and I (also on the newspaper staff) were not amused. Accompanying the cartoon was an op-ed of sorts decrying "Black" behavior at parties, and Black students drafted and signed a petition condemning the piece. We were at first buoyed by the number of student allies who immediately expressed their support. But things got sticky when those allies wanted to add their names to the petition, and we held fast to the notion that a petition from "We, the Black students" should be signed by . . . well, *the Black students*. It went back and forth. Feelings were hurt. We held our ground, suggesting that sympathetic parties start another petition, add a rainbow coalition of outrage to the voices of protest. That didn't go over so well. We were called "reverse racists." The principal called me into her office and gently asked that as student body president, I lead the charge to amend the petition so that White students could sign it. I declined politely. Later that day, the newspaper advisor explained to me and a friend that it was one big misunderstanding and had not been done to offend and oh-so helpfully added that in her day, minstrel shows were legitimate entertainment. The newspaper editors, genuinely chagrined, issued an apology, and life went on. Or so it seemed.

After the school newspaper incident, my friends and I were no longer at ease, but the discomfort was muted by empowerment lessons imparted by our parents and people like Ms. B., who shared both Oprah and Okonkwo (of Chinua Achebe's *Things Fall Apart* fame) with us in African history class. There was Ms. Z., who had the vision and authority to ~~shove~~ nudge us into extracurricular Black theater. I played Mama in *A Raisin in the Sun* (my chagrin at having to play an "old lady" — with padding! — barely mitigated by the fact that I'd gotten a lead role), and yes, we revisited the dashiki days to dance interpretively to Claude McKay's poem "White Houses" in front of the entire school. We were frequently mortified, but more often filled with confidence and pride. We took pride in knowing our roots (and how to dramatize them), and since my friends and I were a competitive group in a competitive class, the A+s flowed. We envisioned ourselves easing on down the road to a top-tier-college future.

I had a pretty good portfolio of College Material that could open doors at a variety of hallowed halls named after Rich Dead Guys. Here I was—honor roll? Check. Good SAT scores? Check. More activities than I actually had time for? Check. I once calculated my after-school commitments and the time that each needed, and it came out to just under sixty-six hours a week. And that was before I counted weekends. Let the record show that I was undeterred. As a reader of both science fiction and fantasy, I figured it was only a matter of time before I uncovered the secrets of time travel, transmogrification, and magic wardrobes that would allow me to Do It All. Looking at the "me" on paper, how could I not expect to be a desirable candidate in the world of higher learning?

And then I signed up for my first and only college prep meeting with my guidance counselor. He took one look at my list—Northwestern, University of Pennsylvania, Cornell, and SUNY Binghamton—and smiled a smile that didn't quite reach his eyes as he said, "These schools are kind of a reach for you."

A reach? For *me*?

I was a certified, bona fide, flag-waving geek. I assumed it was generally accepted common knowledge. Giving him his smile right back, I left the office feeling a little sad for this man who so obviously didn't know Whom He Was Dealing With.

Growing up with Maya Angelou and Malcolm X, Sweet Honey in the Rock, Black History Month every month of the year in my home, and a rainbow coalition of friends and family meant that I *knew who I was.* (I knew who Zora Neale Hurston was, too.) And where I should apply to college.

I waited for the acceptance letters to roll in.

And they did. For all of us. We wore our status like the alligators emblazoned on our shirts. We were academic superstars, remember?

Apparently, not everyone did. At least, not many of our counterparts remembered that we were the same people who sat next to them in AP classes, occasionally gave homework help, and assisted in decoding the poetic genius of hip-hop's pioneers. When the news spread about our acceptances, all of that didn't matter anymore.

We lost one of our labels just like that.

Suddenly, we were no longer part of the school's elite geekarati.

We were only very, very Black.

"It's just . . . so *wrong,*" sputtered my Don't Free South Africa acquaintance on the phone, who was now more well versed in the nature of injustice. "It's *not fair.* Someone like E., who's worked so hard and is so smart, gets rejected from

Harvard, but all of these Black people get into Ivy League schools."

Excuse me?

"People like me, you mean?" I said sweetly, ever polite. My mom taught me manners, even in the face of extreme jackassishness.

There followed much stammering and blustering, and assurances that, of course, he hadn't meant me.

I realized then and there that the same people who'd asked for my notes were always going to see me as more C– than A+, no matter what the report cards said or how good my notes were. And their parents, grumbling about affirmative action and lowered standards in the same breath, probably fed them those thoughts at the dinner table. And some of the wonderful teachers who quietly but fiercely looked out for us let us know that some of their colleagues felt that way, too.

It broke my heart.

I thought I knew the face of racism. In second grade, a classmate who knew a lot of bad words and very little about personal space followed me daily murmuring *"Nigger-niggernigger"* in my ear. Yeah, that was A Year to Remember. And then there was the way our community welcomed an interracial couple — with a cross-burning. Thankfully, a number of neighbors had led a march and vigil in objection to that heartbreaking display of ignorance.

Now I looked around our school and wondered, "Are *you* like *those* cross-burning, epithet-spitting people?"

My teachers and classmates *knew* me. And still the answer to my question wasn't clear.

It. Broke. My. Heart.

But it didn't take long to open my eyes and see the truth: *It was their problem.*

If they didn't get it; well, that was too bad.

I wasn't going to *try talking to them first.*

I'd gotten into the colleges of my choice because I'd worked every multidimensional bone in my body to get there.

I didn't need to be in AP Bio to know how wrong it is to be reduced and flattened to a color (but I was). I wave my identity flag high and wide, marching-band style (yep, did that, too — polyester uniform and all).

I'm Black. I'm a geek.

And nobody can divide that beautiful partnership.

UNDER BERLIN

G. NERI

Berlin is like a theme park.
You got your Nazi Land—
with its huge war monuments,
stone eagles staring you down,
and gold bricks in the ground
telling you how many Jewish folks
from your building died in the war.
You have your Commie World,
all gray and rectangle blocks
of boring buildings,
old Karl Marx statues,
and leftover parts of the Berlin Wall
standing next to a Starbucks.

Then you got Futurama,
where you can ride around on those weird
Segway people movers,
zipping past gleaming towers
and lit-up pyramids
(like Las Vegas but more classy),
all built in the empty space
where the Wall came down.

It's all interesting, I guess.
We're only here
a year for Daddy's work,
so I can put up with anything —
even starting high school
in a place that never heard of
homecoming.
What makes it okay is the food.
There are these amazing gelato stands
(only eighty cents a scoop!),
bakeries on every corner with sweets
you wouldn't believe,
and the currywurst —
that's bratwurst with curry ketchup —
man, I could eat that *forever.*
I'm thinking of opening
a chain of my own

when we get back to the States.
It's that good.

But there are things that suck, too.
German is *hard,*
and nobody ever smiles and says,
Hey, wassup, girl?
When it's cold,
everybody seems grumpy —
I guess complaining about winter
must be like a national sport here.
And then there're the subways. . . .

Me and my family head down
the subway stairs
past the stone eagles
and homeless musicians,
past the currywurst stand
where we usually get a snack.
No stopping today,
it's wall-to-wall
people —
all Germans —
tall and pale,
towering over me
like Euro-gods with tiny glasses.

"Why can't we take a taxi?" I ask.
"You all gonna pay for it, Reina?" asks Daddy,
his southern twang
more out of place
than we are.
We move slowly across the platform,
pushing into the overcrowded train car.
"Sure, I'll pay,
just as soon as I start my own
currywurst stand."
I can still smell it from here.
My brother, Oscar, laughs. "Yeah, right."
I stare at his pudgy face,
trying not to get squished
by the rush-hour stampede.
"What's so funny?" I say.
Oscar laughs again.
"A black American girl
servin' up German sausage?
Sure, that's not funny
at all."
"I'm not *black*," I say.
An old punk rocker,
all leather and tattoos,
laughs when I say that.
I shoot him a look.

My dad is black,
in a real southern way.
But Mom is a light-skinned Hispanic
from Puerto Rico,
so I'm as black as Obama, I guess,
which is only half.
My bro rolls his eyes. "Sorry.
I meant '*mixed* American.'"
His eyes light up —
"Or how about '*mixed-UP* American'?"
Mom makes a face.
"That doesn't even make sense, Papito."
Oscar shrugs, like she ain't
hip enough to get it.

The doors start to close,
so I give Oscar one last shove
'cause we still sticking out
the train door a bit.
We make it in
as the doors seal shut,
but now he's squashed up
against a pole,
looking like he wished
he didn't have a sister.
"You should thank me

for saving your butt," I say.
"You coulda got cut in two
by them doors.
I heard it happened once."
He's thinking of a comeback.
"I pretty sure your *big* butt
woulda stopped those doors
from closing," he mutters.
I laugh in his face. "Dude,
so weak. Move on
before you embarrass yourself.
Oops, sorry, too late."
Then we ignore each other,
standing like sardines
in a tin can with windows.

Mom's feet ache.
So do mine.
Too much walking here,
not like in the States.
Guess that's why
they ain't all fat here.
All they do is walk
and take the subway,
or the *U-bahn,* as they call it.
I wish we had a car,

but Daddy says the subway
is a good way to
"mingle with the people."
That's the only way
to get into a strange culture,
he says — dive in,
headfirst.
So we ride them,
morning
to night.
No taxis for this *familia.*

The subway's kinda like
watching reality TV —
you see all kinds.
I've seen the clothes change
from season to season since we got here:
shorts and porkpie hats and flip-flops
in summer
become heavy coats and fur caps and boots
by winter.
There's funny-looking people:
hipster artist types trying to act all Euro-cool,
workers reading big ol' novels,
students bopping to their iPods,
tourists looking lost and confused.

But most of all,
old people.
Lots of 'em.
I don't think I ever seen
so many old people before.
Daddy says they ain't that old—
they just look it.
Ex-Communists
who lost their way of life
when the Wall came down.
You'd think they'd be happy,
but the older ones aren't.
They like making your life
miserable
'cause they can't have it their way
anymore.
Daddy says, *Just kill 'em*
with kindness.
But they never smile
or give *us* the time of day.

Daddy looks around for a place
to park our butts.
The train is jam-packed—
no place to go.
But he smiles,

winks at me,
and nods toward
two older women,
all uptight with little glasses
and what they think passes
for style: beige pants, beige jackets,
colorful scarves,
and poofy colored hair.
To me, it seems
they all dress the same,
like they in the same old people's club
or something.
There is one empty seat
between them.
Or at least
Daddy thinks there is.
It's more like a small gap,
but it'll do.
"Honey, it's *on*," he says,
pointing to their row.
"Not funny, Papi," Mom says,
frowning.
I look at the old ladies,
especially the one
with a bright-red mop of Lola hair
who holds a small dog

as sour as she is.
I laugh. "Good luck with *that.*"

Daddy shrugs. "I didn't invent the rules.
I just play the game."
"Some role model," Oscar pipes in,
taking Mom's side.
"Mama's boy," I say.
"Daddy's *girl,*" he says, all cutesy
'cause he knows I hate that.
Daddy puts his hands
on our heads.
"Y'all missed
the freedom-bus protests,
so you have no idea," he says.
Mom clears her throat.
"Papi, you were two years old back then,"
she says, blowing his cover.
Daddy gives her a look and shrugs.
"Just sayin'. Now, let your man
go to work."
He adjusts his tie,
smooths down his goatee,
and heads toward the two old ladies,
all smiles and southern charm.
He tips his invisible hat

and says in his best Alabama-German,
"How y'all doin', *fraw-lines*?"
then motions to the empty spot.
They grimace,
like they just swallowed
something bad.
"*Dan-ka*, ma'ams," he says politely,
not waiting for an answer.
He wiggles between them,
clears his throat,
and waits
for the next move. . . .

I try to make eye contact
to see if I can make him
laugh.
But he doesn't.
He has on
his most saintly face,
like he just got baptized
by the pope.
The ladies are
squirming on either side of him.
Even the dog
is jumpy.
It's like Daddy has a disease

or something.
They're looking around,
trying not to be too obvious
about their discomfort,
but he can't help but rub shoulders
with them.
My guess is they watch
American TV and think
if you sit next to a black man,
it's only a matter of time
before he robs you.
Even if he's wearing a suit,
he could still be one of those
Malcolm X brothers.
Ach, mein Gott!

It's like watching popcorn
pop —
sooner or later
they're gonna blow.
I look at my watch.
Thirty seconds.
Mom catches my eye,
frowning at our game.
I ignore her like I don't know
what she's on about.

It used to bother me
when we first arrived in Berlin.
I mean us getting on the subway.
I know these folks
can't quite figure us out.
Daddy's dark skinned;
Mom's light tan.
Oscar looks like a white boy.
But me, I look like an overcooked
mini Jennifer Lopez with nappy hair.
Back home, we ain't no big thing.
But here, they don't know
what to think.

I think Daddy made up
this game,
to show us not to sweat it —
it's all a big joke.
We're doing
social experiments is all.
"See, America's an immigrant country,"
he told us when we first got here.
"We're used to rubbing shoulders
with all kinds.
But here,
they *never* had immigrants

until recently.
They're just *now* learning. . . ."
Not so well,
as far as I can see.
When the Germans brought the Turks
over to do all the manual labor jobs
fifty years ago,
they probably didn't think
Berlin would turn into
the third-largest Turkish city
in the world!
Seems they're sorry
they opened *that* door now.

"Hey, pup, what's your name?"
Daddy's trying to make nice
with the little mutt
in the red-haired lady's lap.
It growls back.
The lady shushes it,
but when Daddy tries to pet it,
she pulls her dog away
and looks up at the announcement board,
like her stop is coming.
She struggles to get to her feet,

then makes her way
to the door,
out of Daddy's sight.
But I keep my eyes on her.
When she thinks
he can't see her anymore,
she spots an empty seat
and slides in next to a nice-looking
German couple.

Daddy spreads out a little more,
his elbow almost touching
the other lady.
He makes eye contact
with me.
I stick my tongue out,
thinking just one
don't count.
If you can't clear out seats
for all of us, then —

Suddenly, the other lady
takes out her cell phone
and acts like it just rang.
Pretends

she can't hear
and has to get up
to walk to another part
of the train for better reception.
But I happen to know
the phones don't work
down here.
Least mine don't.
Still, she gets points
for her acting.

Daddy smiles
and waves us quickly over.
Mom disapproves
but is too tired to argue.
He stands as we squeeze in,
grateful to be sitting
after all that walking.
"Under a minute —
that's pretty good," he says, leaning over,
waiting for my concession speech.
It ain't coming.
"That last one
should become an actor —
she got mad skills," I say instead.

Me and him crack up,
even as a couple across from us
listens in.
I know they know what we're saying,
but I'm just gonna pretend
they don't.
"People here
sure like to move about,
don't they? These seats
must be bad
or something."
I fiddle with mine,
like it's broken.

Mom frowns again.
"I wish you two wouldn't do that.
If this was Montgomery
or Selma in the sixties,
it wouldn't be so funny,
would it? Back in Puerto Rico —"
Daddy cuts her off. "You sitting,
aren't you?
That's like some southern kung fu move —
take all that bad energy
and rechannel it to advance

the cause."
Mom doesn't buy it.
"I'll give you kung fu, Papi," she says,
holding up her hand
to his face.
But he just smiles
that grin of his,
the one that always
melts her heart.
She shakes her head and
finally cracks a smile, too.
Next thing you know,
he leans down and
they kissing.
How can they do *that*
in public?

We sit for the longest time,
making our way across
Berlin.
Turks are starting to board,
and some of the Germans
get off.
When those two ladies
bust a move for the door,

I smile and wave,
even though they ain't looking
my way.
"See ya next time!" I call out.
Mom playfully slaps my hand.
"Stop it. They can't help it
if your Papi is so handsome
it hurts to sit next to him."
Dad pats his hair
and throws us a grin.

Now a couple of Muslim girls
in head scarves sit next to me.
I gotta admit,
it makes me feel weird,
them having to cover up an' all.
Mom notices my face.
"Want to move?" she whispers.
That's what she likes to call *irony*.
I don't play that game.
My brother leans over.
"You might look good
in one of those scarves, Reina.
Especially the ones
that cover your face."

I take the high road
and ignore him.
Mom's impressed.

Another ten minutes pass
and I look around.
No Germans left—
mostly Turks,
Chinese,
Vietnamese,
Africans,
and us.
They all smiling,
looking around like *this*
is how
it should be.
Talking and laughing,
dancing to a Greek guy
playing his crazy violin for money.
They all just biding their time,
waiting for the Europeans
to accept them for who they are.
But things are changing,
a little too fast for some
and way too slow for others.
But someday,

they'll see:
sometimes
you just gotta squeeze your way in,
rub some shoulders,
and hope
they'll rub back.
For that,
I'd be willing to stand.

Just not next to my brother.

Brotherly Love

FRANCISCO X. STORK

The day I talked to my sister started out as an ordinary Sunday. Papá began yelling at us to get ready two hours before we needed to leave for church. I knew Rosalinda would be staying home because I had heard her battle with Papá earlier that morning. Once a month, Papá reluctantly agreed to let Rosalinda stay home on account of *problemas de mujer.*

"Luis, let's go!" I heard Papá yell all the way from his room. I covered my face with my pillow.

"You all right?" Bernie was standing over my bed. He had a worried look on his face. He and I had shared a room since forever. "You haven't been yourself lately. Is everything okay?"

It was hard to keep things from Bernie. He could read something wrong a mile away. And when he asked how you were, it was difficult not to spill your guts out. But there was no way I could tell him what was bothering me that particular morning. Rosalinda was the only one that could help me.

"I can't go to church today," I said.

"Why?" Bernie asked. "Aren't you feeling well?"

"I just need to stay home — that's all."

Bernie was thoughtful for a few seconds, and then he gave me this look as if he understood that my problem was more mental than physical.

"Luis! Why aren't you up yet? We're late!" Papá's large body seemed to fill up most of the room. He had on his shiny black suit with the usual fully starched white shirt and the blue tie with velvet stripes that our mother had picked for him when she was still alive. On Sundays Papá always reminded me of an undertaker. Papá placed his hands on his hips, and that was the signal for me to get up. I never argued with Papá once he put his hands on his hips.

"Papá," Bernie said softly but firmly, "I think Luis should stay home."

"What's the matter with him?"

I glanced at Bernie and then at Papá. "I'm okay," I said.

"He's sick," Bernie said. "He was up all night coughing." I could have sworn I saw Bernie wink at me.

"I didn't hear nothing," Papá said authoritatively.

"Besides, since when does a little cough keep a real man from doing what he needs to do?"

I glanced up at Papá's face in the hope that he might be joking. But no, when it came to pronouncements on what real men do, Papá never joked.

Bernie was not giving up. I don't know how he did it, but he had mysteriously figured out how important it was for me to stay home that morning. "If Mamá was here, she'd make him stay." I was standing up now. Bernie reached out and placed the palm of his hand on my forehead. "Go ahead and touch him," he said to Papá. "He's burning up."

Papá lifted his hand slightly as if to touch me and then changed his mind. "Both of you guys are a bunch of girls, I swear." Papá waved his hand in disgust. "Go ahead and stay, if you're so sick."

We waited until Papá was out of the room. "Thanks," I said to Bernie.

"Enjoy," he responded.

My sister's bedroom shared a wall with my room. Her door was always closed when she was in there. I knocked, timidly.

"I'm not going." Her voice was unwavering.

"It's me. Papá and Bernie left already."

"Please be so kind as to read the sign on the door."

A Do Not Enter sign hung in the middle of her white door. Below the yellow letters, Rosalinda had scribbled with a red marker: SPECIALLY LITTLE GEEKS. That was a reference to me, her geeky little brother. Spelling was not Rosalinda's strength.

"Are you decent?" I asked.

"No. I'm indecent."

"I need to ask you something. It's really important." There was silence on the other side. I knew that was as close to "Come in" as I was going to get. I turned the knob and opened the door slowly. She was lying horizontally on her bed reading. The novels Rosalinda read usually had shirtless men embracing women with glassy eyes and half-opened mouths, the sure look of some kind of intestinal pain. This book, however, had a familiar black cover.

"You're reading the Bible?" I said in shock. Seeing a Bible in Rosalinda's hands was as unlikely as seeing Papá dancing around the house in a tutu.

"Is that so astonishing?" She rested the open book on her stomach and looked at me, poised to defend herself. Rosalinda and I had constant battles over her reading choices.

"Is that for school?" I already knew the answer to my question, but I needed to warm Rosalinda up with some small talk.

"No, I'm reading Leviticus because I just love the way the guy writes. Of course it's for school."

"Leviticus?"

"Yup. Have you read it? What am I saying? Of course you've read it. You've read everything."

"I'm familiar with it," I said with as much nonchalance as I could muster. "What class?"

"World History." Rosalinda yawned. She'd had her best friend, Petra, for a sleepover, and I knew for a wakeful fact that they had stayed up talking until 3:16 a.m.

"Leave it to Mount Carmel to use the Bible for a history book." I tried to make her laugh, or at least smile, but all I got was another yawn. "By the way, what did you say to Papá to get off from going to church?"

"Cramps. What about you?"

"Bernie told him I had a sore throat."

"Great! You should give your sore throat a rest." She made a "go away" motion with her fingers. "I need to finish this before I have to start cooking Sunday dinner. Cramps aren't going to keep me from that." She lifted the book above her face. When I didn't move, she lowered it again. "Okay, what do you want?"

I sat gingerly on the edge of the bed. She eyed my movements the way a cat eyes an over-friendly dog.

"I have a family question." I hoped I didn't sound too anxious.

She flipped quickly to her side and propped her jaw on the palm of her hand. I guess even a question from your geeky brother is better than Leviticus. "Shoot," she said, pretending she could care less, but I detected interest. "But remember, you get what you pay for."

"Ha, ha!"

"Seriously, could you do my report? It would be a piece of cake for a genius like you. All you have to do is give four examples of how women were treated when Leviticus was written."

"You should ask Papá. He's the real Bible expert in the house. Besides, that's so easy, even *you* can do that," I replied. The foot attached to her long leg reached the small of my back. "Ouch!" I wanted to talk about what was eating me, but it was hard not to jab at her. She was such an easy target.

"Speak now or forever hold your peace," she commanded.

"Is that piece as in P-I-E-C-E?"

It took Rosalinda a few moments to spell the word in her head. "That's hilarious." She flashed me a fake grin.

What can I tell you? I'm a moron when I'm stressed. I cleared my throat. It was time to get serious. "It's about Bernie," I managed to say.

"What about him?" Her immediate and concerned response confirmed for me once and for all that Bernie was her favorite brother. Bernie was beyond reproach. She happened to be right, but it still hurt a little, the way she was always so ready to defend him.

"Why do you think that he never goes out with anyone? I

mean all your friends are always after him. Petra has orgasmic spasms whenever he even glances in her direction, which is not often. And she's supposed to be sizzling."

"Okay, okay. Hold on a second. Let's go through what you said step by step. Let's *ANAL*ize things, as you like to say. What do you know about 'orgasmic spasms'?"

"Everyone knows about orgasmic spasms. It's common knowledge."

She lifted her eyebrows. They were stuck up there for about ten seconds.

She sighed. "You're how old? Thirteen?"

"Fourteen next month."

"Fourteen going on forty!" She sighed.

"Okay, okay, you don't have to get a cow over it."

"It's 'have a cow,' not 'get a cow,' and you shouldn't be quoting Bart if you've never watched the show."

"Who's Bart?"

"I rest my case." She sat up and scooted to the head of the bed, where she propped a pillow behind her. "Why doesn't Bernie go out with anyone?" She scrounged her eyebrows in my direction. I could tell that she wasn't pondering the question. She was penetrating my skull, trying to decipher the gray hieroglyphics that twisted chaotically in there. "Now, why would you ask such a question?"

"I just find it strange. He's eighteen, extremely handsome,

has an after-school job at Papá's garage, so he has money, and I've never seen him go out with anybody."

"And that bothers you because . . ."

"I'm worried about him?"

She gave me her bull-detector grin. "Try again," she said.

I took a deep breath. "Do you think he might be — ?"

"No," she cut me off. "He's not." Then she rubbed her chin à la Sherlock Holmes. "But it is very interesting that *you* should be asking me that."

I gush of hot blood rushed from the tip of my toes to the top of my head. I started to get up.

"Wait. Sit." She waited for me to obey. I sat on the bed reluctantly. "I'm going to answer your question."

"What question?" I asked.

"Why Bernie doesn't go out with girls."

Oh, that question.

"Bernie is a noble kind of guy."

"You mean as in he moves around a lot?"

"What?"

"Oh, *noble*. I thought you said *mobile*."

"You are such an idiot." She paused to collect herself and then continued: "First of all, Bernie goes out with more girls then you know about. He just doesn't date girls from Mount Carmel. Why, you ask? Most girls at Mount Carmel are not like *moi*. Most of them are like Petra — you know: beautiful but traditional. What do you think would happen to Petra, for example, if Bernie asked her out?"

"They'd have to call the coroner?"

"Do you want a serious answer to your question or not?"

I nodded. The focus of the conversation had shifted from me to Bernie, so I was fine.

Rosalinda's face was suddenly serious. "The reason Bernie doesn't ask Petra out, or any one of countless girls at Mount Carmel, is because those kind of girls want a serious relationship and Bernie is waiting until the absolute right girl comes along. He doesn't like to date the same girl more than once or twice. If he dates a girl more than twice, that's probably the one he'll marry. Besides, he knows that if he went out with anyone from Mount Carmel, that poor girl would be a goner, heart-forever-broken, not the same again, ever." She waited a quick moment and then went on, "And even if that poor girl ever managed to eventually marry someone else, she would be doing so out of a sense of hopeless resignation. You follow?"

It took me a few moments to fully understand what she was saying, and then I nodded. Rosalinda for once in her life was right. All the girls at Mount Carmel were already half in love with Bernie. If he went out with them, they would want to bear him children right there on the spot. Shoot, if he was a sheik and they were only one of a thousand wives, they'd stand in line and take a number. "I follow," I said in agreement.

It was the right time, I thought, to take my inquiry one step further. "It's just that there are some things about him. . . ."

"Such as?"

"He cooks. He even bakes. He makes cupcakes with pink frosting."

Rosalinda laughed. "Oh, I get it. And real men don't do that, right?"

"Not according to Papá, they don't. Real Mexican men don't cook or bake."

"Yeah, right, if it were up to Papá, I'd have to do all the cooking and dishwashing and cleaning around here. Thank God there's at least one person that helps me." She shot me her deadliest killer glance. "By the way, who eats the cupcakes?"

"Not all of them," I answered guiltily. Then, I added, "And he's always going with you to the mall to help you shop."

"Well, sometimes I need a man's advice."

"Why? Because you want to impress Manny Luongo?" Manny Luongo was the quarterback at Mount Carmel and, next to my brother, the hottest guy at school. I had just the night before discovered that Rosalinda had a thing for him.

"How . . . ?" she said, eyes narrowing. "You were eavesdropping on me and Petra again, weren't you?"

"That's not all," I said, trying to change the subject. "Bernie drives a light-blue Prius!"

"So?" Rosalinda asked, mystified.

"Papá says it's a sissy's car."

"Oh, here we go again. Papá. Papá. Papá. Do you believe everything Papá says? You think I believe everything Papá says or the nuns at school tell me? I'm an independent woman, buddy. You should try that kind of thinking yourself instead of accepting everything that Papá says as gospel truth. Besides, who washes that baby-blue car about twenty times a week, which is almost as many times as he takes a shower?"

"I don't like to see him drive a dirty car. It doesn't reflect well on the family. And I take lots of showers because I like to smell clean."

"And you use my moisturizer because . . ."

Once again blood made its customary trip from toe to hair follicles. How did Rosalinda know? I was so careful. "It's good for pimples," I mumbled.

"And who reads *Vogue*?" She was looking straight at me.

"You do."

"And who else?"

"Only when I'm in the bathroom."

"Ewwww! No wonder you spend hours in there. Have you ever seen him even open that magazine?"

"Who?"

"Bernie. Who else are we talking about?"

She was annoyingly right yet again. I had never seen Bernie read *Vogue*. "Why does he buy it, then?" I asked, confused.

"He buys it for us, for you and me. Mostly he buys it for you. I told him once I preferred *Cosmo*, but he said, and I quote, 'Luis likes the fashions in *Vogue*.' Are you getting all this?"

I was stunned. I was a pretty smart guy. I never got a B in my life. I was also very perceptive. I could tell if Rosalinda was wearing a blouse from Abercrombie and Fitch or Anthropologie. But it never occurred to me, never, not for one microsecond, that Bernie bought *Vogue* for me to read, which I did every month, religiously, from cover to cover, and not just when I was in the bathroom.

I stopped. I blinked. Then I rubbed my right eye with my index finger. Rosalinda never cleaned her room, and dust was always flying everywhere. "Remember when Papá found the computer open to the website on baking recipes? He was so mad at Bernie. God hates a *maricón*, he said. Especially a Mexican one." My voice was low. I could hardly say the word. It had sounded nasty when Papá said it, but it sounded ten times worse hearing myself say it.

Rosalinda folded her legs and then crawled on her knees to where I was. Before I could do anything, she grabbed me by the shoulder and planted a big wet kiss on my cheek.

"Okay, okay," I said softly, pretending to pull away, "don't get a cow."

She sat on her haunches on top of the bed, not letting go of me. "And what did Bernie do when Papá said that?"

I couldn't speak. There was a lump in my throat the size

and texture of one of those Mexican limes that Bernie liked to squeeze on his chicken soup. "He told him not to say that kind of stuff ever again. That it was not something Jesus Christ would ever say. That it was a bunch of *mierda,* and that God—that God made all kinds of Mexican guys."

She moved closer to me and sat on the edge of the bed. "Have you ever, before that day, heard Bernie use that word?"

I shook my head.

"You know why he did that?"

I shook my head again.

"It was like he was defending someone, wasn't it?" She was almost whispering in my ear.

I nodded.

"He did it for you. He was defending you. You! Luis. Our geeky little Mexican guy, made just right by God."

The green lime that had been stuck in my throat exploded, and I was suddenly crying. I buried my head in Rosalinda's chest. I don't know how long we sat there next to each other. Finally, I wiped my eyes on my arm. Rosalinda lifted a corner of her chartreuse T-shirt to dry my cheeks. "Bright colors make you look fat," I said.

She smiled and rubbed the back of my head. "Told you I needed a guy's advice, didn't I? Now, get out of here. Go to the bathroom and read your magazine."

I stood up.

"But don't take forever," she warned.

I looked at her one more time and smiled. Then I slowly walked out.

I noticed, as I was walking to my room, that my steps were lighter, so much lighter.

LEXICON

NAOMI SHIHAB NYE

Hearts, like doors, will (open) with ease
to very, very little keys,
and don't forget that two of these
are "Thank you, sir," and "If you please."
                                    — *Traditional*

1.
Certain words
got lost on their way —
why should they pull us
down their twisted paths?

Using them feeds them.
War is *raw,* backward and forward.

Terror contains *rot* and *tore*.
Well, of course.
It would not be filled
with *toast* or *lamp*.

Because my Arab father said,
I love you, habibi,
darling was everywhere.
Sweetness emanating from trees.
Mint in your tea?
Ahlan wa sahlan — you are all welcome.
Friends, strangers, came right in.
Sat in a circle, poured, and stirred.
Teacups steaming on an oval tray.

Being a good example —
why not?
(I was half-baked, mix of East and West,
balancing flavors.)
When they said, *May we tell you about Jesus?*
my father said, *He was my next-door neighbor!*

Because my father said, *Eye of my eye,*
heart of my heart, I felt surrounded —
soft love cocoon. He went outside to
smell the air. It spoke to him.

He crossed the creek,
took a turn.

How much you could own without owning.
Soft hope tucked into branches.
Down the block and up the hill.

My friend's dad said,
Let's get rolling, girls.
He was brusque, tough.
He drank beer and spat.
You're not leaving this house
till you finish your work.
My father's tongue had no *bitch*
hiding under it.

Mine said *friend* to everyone.
You don't even know her, Dad.
I'll know her sooner if I call her friend.

He was Facebook before it existed.
Only Arab on the block,
on the street, in the town,
he ran for president of the PTA.
Maybe not, said my mom.
But he won.

All his friends voted for him.
The Italians, the French Canadians.
If someone said, *I never met an Arab before!*
he would beam.
If someone spoke rudely,
he softened instead of hardening.
Oh, my, he'd say. *Let's start this
conversation again.*

Where have you gone, Daddy?
I need my personal Arab in a world of headlines.
I need your calm, loving voice like a rug on all the floors.

He hated chaos,
fighting,
wars.
He said, *Let's get more information.*
Man of gentle words,
could we bury nasty ones
in a graveyard now?

Then the earth would be polluted.

Tie them into sacks,
pitch them into lakes?
Then the lakes would be strange.

Words that never helped us?

Holding someone above.
Words aimed in anger.
Words that made walls.

Maybe we need a giant campfire,
all the dry twigs of sad words piled on top.
Light them carefully, say good-bye.
Fold your hands as they sizzle and fly, ash into air.
This will not be a fire to cook anything on.

2.
We need more words like
Comfortable
Bedrock
Pillow
Cake

Words that make us part of a whole.
Compass
Time
Chickadee
Shadow
Errand

Dreamboat
Canvas words.
Words with hems and pockets.
Umbrella, flashlight, milk.
Pencil, blizzard, song.
Words like parks to sit in.
Bench words. Did you ever notice how
pleasant and *pleasure* have *please* in them?
Except for that final *e,* which is waiting for
everybody to wrap their tongues around it.

In Geneva, Switzerland, I saw the longest bench
in the world. It stretched the length
of a block or two—
green with little snowdrifts
piled against the back—
no one sitting on it just then.
I wondered if my father ever sat on it.
Dreaming of words,
merci,
sesame,
I wanted to stay, sitting quietly,
soaking in memory,
till spring washed over
everyone, visible, invisible,

watching everyone pass,
in the neutral country,
the second United Nations city,
holding the thoughts.

Remembering my father's daily sweetness,
the way some people make you feel better
just by stepping into a room.
He loved the freshness of anything —
crisp cucumbers, the swell of a new day.
The way skin feels after being washed.
I'm happy to see you!
The day just got happier.

But dying, this lover of life said sadly,
My dilemma is large.
Nothing had become the world he dreamed of.
He wanted
simple times, people making room
for fun, for words.
Saying *darling* to fresh minutes lined up.
Shookrun — thank you — to legs strong enough to walk.
Shookrun to light coming over the fields.
Shookrun to light touching the houses.
Shookrun to everyone we haven't met yet.

Especially the nice ones.
Yes to all forgotten ones.

And then there would be language worth trading.
Words deserved by human beings, all deserving respect.
Coins and plums and an endless kiss
no one saw you get or give.

ABOUT THE CONTRIBUTORS

CHERRY CHEVA (full name: Cherry Chevapravatdumrong) is originally from Ann Arbor, Michigan. She is the author of two novels, *She's So Money* and *DupliKate*, and the co-author, with Alex Borstein, of *It Takes a Village Idiot, and I Married One*. She is a writer and producer for *Family Guy* and lives in Los Angeles. "A lot of people watching the *Family Guy* credits think my name is fake," says Cherry. "It's not. It's just Thai."

VARIAN JOHNSON is the author of *Saving Maddie, My Life as a Rhombus*, and *A Red Polka Dot in a World Full of Plaid*. He was born and raised in Florence, South Carolina, and attended the University of Oklahoma, where he received a BS in civil engineering. He also received an MFA in writing for children and young adults from the Vermont College of Fine Arts and lives in Austin, Texas. "I was the typical high-school geek," he says. "I played the baritone in the marching band, was a member of the Academic Challenge Team, and counted my Hewlett-Packard 48G calculator as one of my most prized possessions."

G. NERI, author of *Ghetto Cowboy, Chess Rumble, Yummy: The Last Days of a Southside Shorty,* and *Surf Mules,* is a storyteller, filmmaker, artist, and digital-media producer. He taught animation and storytelling to inner-city teens in Los Angeles with the groundbreaking group AnimAction, producing more than three hundred films. "I'm Creole, Filipino, and Mexican—or as I like to call it, Crefilican. On top of that, my daughter is also German. If America's the melting pot of the world, then we're perfect examples of how diverse this country really is." Although he lives on the Gulf Coast of Florida, he and his family spent a year in Berlin, where he was often able to corral extra subway seats.

NAOMI SHIHAB NYE was born in St. Louis, Missouri. Her father was a Palestinian refugee, her mother an American of German and Swiss descent. Naomi grew up in Jerusalem and San Antonio, Texas. She is considered one of the leading female poets of the American Southwest and is the author of *Habibi*, an award-winning novel for children. She received her BA from Trinity University in San Antonio and continues to live and work there. "Writing is the great friend that never moves away," says Naomi.

MITALI PERKINS, author of *Bamboo People, Secret Keeper, Monsoon Summer,* and other novels for young readers, was born in India and immigrated to the States with her parents and two sisters when she was seven. Bengali-style, the three sisters' names rhyme: *Sonali* means "gold," *Rupali* means "silver," and *Mitali* means "friendly." "I had to live up to my name because we moved so much," Mitali says. "I've lived in India, Ghana, Cameroon, England, New York, Mexico, California, Bangladesh, Thailand, and now, in Newton, Massachusetts."

OLUGBEMISOLA RHUDAY-PERKOVICH wrote *8th Grade Superzero,* an International Reading Association Notable Book for a Global Society. She is featured in several books on writing: *Real Revision, Seize the Story, Wild Ink,* and *Keep Calm and Query On,* and is a contributor to the essay collection *Break These Rules.* She has a master's in educational technology with a concentration in English education. "I was the new kid at school many times over, in more than one country," says Olugbemisola. "I now live with my family in Brooklyn, where I write, make things, and need more sleep."

DEBBIE RIGAUD was born in Manhattan, but the Rigaud family packed up the kids and headed to East Orange, New Jersey. "My parents never fully transitioned to Jersey living," says Debbie. "My childhood was happily spent heading back to Brooklyn for doctors' visits, summer vacations, ripe plantains—every excuse in the book." She has written for many magazines, including *Entertainment Weekly, Seventeen, Vibe, Cosmo Girl!, Essence, Heart & Soul,* and *Trace* magazine in London. Debbie is also the author of *Perfect Shot,* a novel for teens, and lives in Bermuda.

FRANCISCO X. STORK works in Boston as a lawyer for a state agency that develops affordable housing. He was born in Monterrey, Mexico, to Ruth Arguelles, a single mother from a middle-class family in Tampico, a city on the Gulf of Mexico. He is the author of five novels: *The Way of the Jaguar, Behind the Eyes, Marcelo in the Real World, The Last Summer of the Death Warriors,* and *Irises.* "Part of me left Mexico when I was nine, and part of me is still there," says Francisco.

GENE LUEN YANG is the author and illustrator of *American Born Chinese* and *Prime Baby,* and co-creator of *The Eternal Smile, Level Up,* and *Avatar: The Last Airbender — The Promise.* He was born in the San Francisco Bay Area after his father emigrated from Taiwan and his mother from Hong Kong. "In fifth grade, my mother took me to our local bookstore, where she bought me my first Superman comic book," he says, explaining his lifelong love of the genre. Yang attended the University of California, Berkeley, majoring in computer science with a minor in creative writing, and received his master's in education from Cal State, Hayward, where he wrote his thesis on using comics in education. He teaches high school in the San Francisco Bay Area.

DAVID YOO lived in Seoul, South Korea, from age three to eight, during which time he learned how to curse fluently in Korean. From eight years old to now, he is a lifelong New

Englander, and the author of *The Detention Club, Stop Me If You've Heard This One Before, Girls for Breakfast,* and, most recently, a collection of essays for adults, *The Choke Artist: Confessions of a Chronic Underachiever.* He teaches in the MFA program at Pine Manor College and has a column in *KoreAm Journal,* in which he says he "recounts the stupidest thing he did the previous month."